HIS FOR A WEEK:
DEVASTATED

EM BROWN

Kimani:
He's back. The man who bought, ravaged and
tormented me.

I can't fall for him again. He's wrong for me in so many
ways. His last act of punishment cost me my job, and I
don't know that I can forgive him.

And yet his touch leaves me…devastated.

His For A Week:
DEVASTATED

Chapter One

"I don't know about that," Sam Green, the editor of the *San Francisco Tribune*, replied to Kimani Taylor's suggestion. "A profile on Gordon Lee? It sounds like a fluff piece, and we don't do that kind of stuff."

Kimani, sitting on the other side of Sam's desk in his office overlooking downtown San Francisco, persisted. "The paper did a profile of the mayor of San Francisco last year."

"San Francisco is our base. You know our East Bay section is limited as it is."

"The election of mayor to the eighth largest city in California is a big deal."

Sam eyed her carefully, seeking her ulterior motivation. "You seem to want to do this as badly as you wanted to do that scoop on the Scarlet Auction."

Kimani lowered her eyes for a moment. Her undercover story of the Scarlet Auction, in which women sold themselves for a week to the highest bidder, had yet to be published, at the request of the district attorney's office, which had begun an investigation into the Scarlet Auction and didn't want to sound any alarm bells before they had collected enough information to bring charges.

It was actually no longer Kimani's story. She had

become too involved, thanks to the man who had "bought" her. Benjamin Lee.

In case Sam believed she was biased in favor of Gordon, Benjamin's uncle, she added, "I'm not suggesting we do a profile just on Gordon Lee, but all the other candidates in the Oakland mayoral race. So it's fair."

Sam steepled his fingertips. "That's a lot of real estate you're asking for."

"I don't think the people know the real Gordon Lee. They see him as a boring bureaucrat, but he's more than that."

"And you know this because you're well acquainted with the guy?"

"Not so well that I can't remain impartial, but if you're worried about that, I don't mind doing the work, the research, the writing, and handing it off to someone else so they can have the byline."

"That's very philanthropic of you, but you're not going to get very far in your career with charity. You know that there are very few jobs in journalism these days. It's a dog-eat-dog world now."

Kimani appreciated the advice from her mentor and former graduate school of journalism instructor, but until she made things right with Gordon Lee, guilt would forever gnaw at her.

She had screwed up. Badly. Royally. If she had never told Sam of the text that had come across Ben's cellphone when she was using it, a text that was a private communication from one of Ben's business colleagues, Sam wouldn't have thought to write an article about Oakland Forward, a political action committee formed by local developers and business interests in support of Gordon Lee for mayor.

By law, independent expenditures such as Oakland Forward could not coordinate with the campaign of an individual candidate that it was supporting, but because Ben was family to the candidate, Gordon was implicated. As a result of the article, the state's Fair Political Practices Commission had launched an investigation into Gordon's campaign. While Ben had been the one to suggest the formation of a political action committee, he had stepped away from the PAC before its official formation. It was not his fault that the new chairman of the PAC had chosen to share some good news with Ben.

It had been an oversight. Kimani was sure of it, but in her initial skepticism of Ben and her eagerness to give Sam what he wanted, she had betrayed Ben.

In her defense, she didn't know what Sam had planned to do with the bit of information she had unwittingly passed on to him. But that didn't exonerate her. She could've done better. And even though she had gotten what she had set out to achieve—landing her dream job as a reporter for the *San Francisco Tribune*—her dream-come-true felt miserable. And even Ben's forgiveness would not wash away the pit in her stomach.

The fact that he *hadn't* forgiven her, however, did

make her feel worse. He hadn't returned any of her calls. After trying him several times, in all the ways that she knew how, she had written him an old-fashioned letter addressed to his office in San Francisco.

His receptionist had said Ben was back in China, with no word of when he would return to California. Kimani didn't know if the letter would reach him, and if he would read it if it did. She had omitted her name in the return address to bolster the chances that he would at least open the envelope. But after seeing it was from her, maybe he would just cast it into the nearest wastebasket.

She had ceased trying to contact him after sending the letter. At this point, she didn't expect to ever hear from him again. And she didn't blame him for not wanting to talk to her.

But even though she reminded herself each day of the benefits of putting Ben out of her mind, deep down, a part of her still wished he would call. Even if it was to put some closure to the end of their brief but emotional relationship.

Relationship wasn't quite the right word. It was four and a half days of sex. The guy had "bought" her for a fling because he had been the only guy at the cabin without a date. He'd wanted a fucktoy for himself.

Somehow, in the course of their time together, she had developed feelings for Ben. And it wasn't just because he was the nicest compared to the other three men she considered racist, misogynist, or naïve frat boys. She had to admit that being with Ben was exciting, exhilarating, enlightening, and fun. Not to mention he'd taken her to the most amazing sexual heights, always pushing her body to the brink when she thought there was no way she could take any more, when she thought she would crack, but instead found greater and greater euphoria.

Now, her vibrator had never looked so boring. It was hard not to relive those moments bound in his shibari, pinned to his hardness, and falling to pieces at his touch. For a while, she had avoided pleasuring herself so that she wouldn't drift back to those memories, but the memories had a way of coming after her anyway. She had purchased the Womanizer and the LELO SONA, both of which Ben had used on her their first night in his penthouse, but it still wasn't the same. The fact that *he'd* wielded them had made all the difference.

"You want me to undo the best weave I've ever done?" Keisha had asked when Kimani had gone to see her a few days ago. "Not that you weren't a fine sister to begin with, but this here weave makes you look hotter than Beyonce."

Kimani hadn't been thrilled to see the braids with gold sewn in taken apart, but she remembered all too vividly Ben's reaction to her weave, and how he had taken her in the bathroom of the coffee house afterward.

"I got a new job as a reporter for the *San Francisco*

Tribune," Kimani had explained. "I need a look that's less flashy and more professional."

Keisha had put a hand on her hip. "You saying my weave doesn't look professional?"

"No, it's just..."

"You can't look gorgeous and professional at the same time?"

"I just want a different look. More 'me.'"

Keisha raised a doubtful eyebrow. "Un-hunh."

"What's that supposed to mean?"

"It means he ain't out of your system, is he?"

"Who are you referring to?" Kimani stalled, knowing that Keisha more than likely referred to Ben.

"That Asian guy. You still got a case of rice fever."

"I don't have rice fever."

"I heard you only had two dates with Marcus, and that brother is *fine,* so I figure you—"

"Look, Marcus is a nice guy, but—"

Keisha put up a hand. "Hold up. You don't have to say anything more. 'Nice' says it all. This guy from Hong Kong must be something for you to turn down Marcus. You don't even have to date the brother. Just sleep with him. I heard the brother is so damn hung, his dick could dig its way to China."

Kimani rolled her eyes. "You going to do my hair or what?"

"Un-hunh. Just like I figured."

Though Kimani knew Keisha was just trying to bait her, she took it. "Figured what?"

"That you ain't over him."

"Just because I don't want to talk about him doesn't mean anything."

"And I thought you were smart, being a Stanford grad and all. It's obvious that *because* you don't want to talk about this guy, means your feelings for him are still raw—that and the fact that you aren't even considering doing it with Marcus, because any woman in her right mind would do it with Marcus."

"Just do my hair. Please."

Keisha had let it go after that, but Kimani had to acknowledge that, once again, Keisha's insight was right. Maybe the woman was able to read minds somehow through her contact with a person's hair.

Talking about Ben only reminded her of her pain, and the emptiness she felt that he was no longer in her life. She had thought herself too smart for that old adage about not knowing a good thing till it's gone. She liked and understood Passenger's "Let Her Go," but she never thought to experience it firsthand. Yet, she hadn't realized the full extent of her feelings for Ben until everything was over between them. And now she missed him.

She even missed the way he made her drink green tea. She had never been much of a tea drinker, and green was probably her least favorite flavor. But just yesterday she had found herself ordering a green tea at the local coffee shop.

She had rationalized to herself that she couldn't fall for a guy like Ben. A guy willing to buy a woman for sex. Men like that had issues. She still believed that to be the case, but somehow, she had been lucky enough to find the one in a hundred who wasn't so bad. And who happened to be amazing in bed. It was like something out of a fantasy, or one of those erotic romance novels that Claire liked to read.

In real life, fairy tales don't always come true. In real life, rakes don't suddenly become relationship material because they found the "right" woman. In real life, a desperate journalist still trying to pay off her student loans wouldn't be dating a billionaire. And if she was dating a ridiculously wealthy man, he was unlikely to be the man of her dreams.

So now that Ben was out of the picture, her life was back to normal.

After taking out the braids, Keisha had taken a flat iron to Kimani. The resulting style would require more maintenance, but Kimani welcomed the extra labor. She didn't want too much time alone with her thoughts.

"Look, we owe it to the guy," Kimani said to Sam.

Sam narrowed his eyes. "What do you mean?"

"That piece you ran about Oakland Forward."

"I reported only the facts."

"And because the FPPC is investigating, Gordon Lee is taking a hit in the polls, even if he's innocent. In the court of public opinion, you're not innocent until proven guilty. Just the *possibility* of wrongdoing has an effect."

"It'll sort itself out. If Lee is innocent, the FPPC investigation will prove that."

"But will the investigation reach that conclusion before the election?"

"I know this is going to sound callous, but it's not our problem."

"You could have waited to publish that article. Until we had more to go on."

She held her breath during his silence. She had never before challenged her mentor, the man she owed her job to.

"Okay," he acknowledged. "Maybe I jumped the gun a little because I knew ownership was talking soon. They've been pretty tight-lipped about the future of the *Tribune* recently, but one of the owners did let slip to me that there's a chance the paper won't shut down. They're waiting for the ink to dry on a deal before releasing any details."

Kimani perked up. "That's great! So, can we do a profile of Gordon Lee or not?"

Sam thought some more before answering, "Do it. But I'm trusting your professionalism and the fact that you're not going to let personal biases influence your work."

"You don't have to give me the byline."

"Work with Alvarez on the profiles. You'll have to do all the candidates, even the ones who have zero chance of winning."

Kimani was so happy she would have hugged Sam if the table wasn't between them. It was better she didn't, because she didn't want to appear too emotional in front of him.

Now that she had gotten Sam's go-ahead, the harder part remained: convincing Gordon Lee to grant her an interview. She didn't know what Ben had told him about her part in the Oakland Forward article, but she bet none of it was in her favor.

However, if she could write this profile of him and give the public a glimpse of the man she had seen when she'd been with Ben, it might alleviate some of the damage done by the ongoing FPPC investigation. She wanted to write this piece as badly as she'd wanted to write one on the Scarlet Auction.

As Kimani rode the municipal light rail back home after staying at the office past eight o'flock, she received a text from her roommate, Marissa:

> Have to work late. Thinking
> of going to The Lair. Will let
> you know

The Lair was the BDSM club Marissa used to frequent. Kimani was glad to hear that Marissa might head to The Lair since she hadn't been active there since her experience with the Scarlet Auction.

By the time Kimani got off at her Muni stop, the streets leading to the duplex she and Marissa rented together were fairly dark. An elderly couple, James and Michael, lived in the upstairs unit and were rarely home because they enjoyed traveling. Currently they were on an Alaskan cruise, scarfing down at the all-you-can-eat buffet, their favorite part of cruising.

As Kimani fumbled through her purse for her house keys, she had the odd sensation that she was being watched. She looked behind her but saw only a neighbor across the street walking her dog. Glad that she wasn't alone, Kimani found her keys and let herself in.

After taking off her shoes and going through the refrigerator to find a snack, she looked through the mail Marissa had left on the table. Amidst the bills and credit card applications was a letter addressed to her with no return address. Kimani opened the envelope and pulled out a single sheet of paper. It was blank except for six typed words:

I KNOW WHERE YOU LIVE, BITCH.

Chapter Two

The naked, petite woman dangled from the ceiling of the dark room. On occasion, a flash of blue from the strobe lights downstairs in the bar area would permeate the room. An experienced submissive, Yuki could spend hours in predicament bondage. The rope wrapped her upper body in asymmetric formation from the top of one shoulder to the bottom of the other, squeezing down on one breast while the other orb was pulled upward.

Benjamin Lee stared at his shibari handiwork on the woman. Though he didn't favor waifs and women who looked far younger than their age—Yuki was twenty-eight but could easily pass for jailbait—he had specifically chosen Yuki out of the many submissives making eyes at him in the Tokyo BDSM club because she was different from Kimani in almost every way. Yuki had poker-straight hair—currently tied back messily in a ponytail—alabaster skin, and, except for her breasts, had a straight and skinny figure.

"*Irete kudasai*," she said with large, imploring eyes.

When Ben did not respond immediately, she tried English instead. "Fuck me."

Fluent in Japanese, Ben didn't need the translation. He hadn't reacted because he had been distracted, thinking about the different ways he had wanted to tie Kimani in suspension bondage. Her legs spread apart. With and without a crotch rope. Upside down. Right-side up. One leg stretched skyward.

Fuck that.

Unzipping his pants, Ben grabbed a condom and went to stand behind Yuki. After sheathing his cock, he pulled her hips toward him and thrust himself into her.

She cried out in Japanese as his cock entered her with ease, for she was dripping wet thanks to their earlier foreplay, which had included nose hooks, a favorite of hers.

He pounded away at her, gripping her hips tightly because she barely weighed a hundred pounds and would have flown across the room. Unlike Kimani, who had more substance, more muscle. He would have liked to test how hard Kimani could take it. The anger still lingered, so he probably wouldn't have held back if it was she and not Yuki speared upon his cock.

Bloody hell.

It had been weeks since he had left California. Why was he still thinking about her?

He drilled himself into Yuki as if doing so could drive Kimani out of his head.

For a brief moment, as his orgasm rattled his bones and burst through his cock, all thought evaporated. A beautiful and blinding bliss overcame him.

But it never lasted. No matter how many times he

sought that destination, he always ended up back where he started.

"You got yourself a cute little *joro*," May said, nursing an umetini in one of the booths near the club's bar, where Ben joined her after seeing Yuki come and releasing her from the ropes.

Across from them on a large screen, a scene with two BBWs played. All about the main floor of the club hung cages in which women, mostly or all naked, writhed and posed.

Of his three sisters, he would only ever attend a sex club with May, the third of the four Lee children, who was currently on an unwanted "break" from her relationship. Their father had never liked the fact that May was gay, and because Ben had had his own issues with the head of the Lee family, he and May had formed a bond growing up.

Of her siblings, May looked the least like her mother and more like their father, with her round face and flatter nose. She wore her hair short with the tips colored purple.

"Yuki's very open to women," Ben said as he ordered kuusu on ice from the waitress clad in a short kimono that didn't fully cover her arse.

May raised her brows. "What happened to ordering water or green tea?"

"It's not like I never drink," Ben replied. "And if you plan on reading things into everything I do, this is the last time I let you accompany me to Tokyo."

But May wasn't afraid of his threats. "We sure are

surly since coming home."

He gave her a stern stare.

Still undaunted, May only leaned in closer. Women were like bloodhounds catching the scent of a fox when it came to acquiring knowledge they felt men were withholding from them. "So who was she?"

"Who?"

"You had some girl while you were in San Francisco."

"I didn't have anyone," he replied, then decided to throw her a bone in the hopes that it would be enough to satisfy her curiosity. "She was just a fucktoy."

A fucktoy he had called his pet for four, nearly five fucked-up days.

May sat back and eyed him carefully. "What was her name?"

The waitress came back with his drink, handing it to him instead of setting it down on the table so that their fingers would have to touch. Noticing, May rolled her eyes.

"You have a target on your back, brother," May said. "The girls here probably all think you're some prospective *mitsugu kun*... Are you?"

Her question surprised him. May knew that unless a woman was family, Ben didn't tend to keep any woman around for long, and he certainly wasn't anyone's *mitsugu kun*, or sugar daddy.

"This fucktoy in California. What's her name?"

"Why do you want to know?" he returned.

"Just curious."

"Liar." If he gave her a name, she would head straight to the internet to look up all that she could on Kimani Taylor.

She wrinkled her nose as he imbibed his kuusu, a distilled alcohol not unlike single-malt scotch.

"The fact that you won't give up her name means she was more than just a fucktoy," May shot back.

"I knew her all of four and a half days. She was just a fucktoy."

An expensive fucktoy that had cost him two hundred thousand dollars. After the stunt Jake had pulled, he ought to have asked for his money back, but he didn't want to have anything more to do with the wanker. And with the net worth of the Lee family at thirteen billion dollars, two hundred thousand was nothing to fret over.

Except Ben didn't treat real money like play money. He opted for the finer things in life but had heard enough stories of how his grandparents could only afford to purchase meat for dinner once a week to understand that wealth was something to cherish, not squander on frivolous purchases.

Paying two hundred thousand dollars to have sex with a woman for a week was frivolous. But it hadn't felt frivolous at the time. He'd told himself that it was partly because he hadn't trusted Jake with her. He was being a bloody good Samaritan.

But that didn't explain everything. If he had only been acting out of altruism, he could have also purchased Claire, the other woman Jake had bid on and won through the Scarlet Auction. But he had only wanted Kimani. And to seal the deal without any hesitation from Jake, he had offered an exorbitant amount of money.

"Just like Yuki," he finished.

May, however, wasn't finished. She returned his pointed stare. "Now who's the liar?"

He downed the rest of the kuusu and considered calling it night, but May wasn't done challenging him.

"Growing up, we told each other everything. You've never kept anything from me before."

"I don't tell you about every woman I choose to fuck, and you don't tell me about every woman *you* choose to fuck."

"True. But if you wanted to know the name of one, I'd tell you."

He could see that she wasn't going to let it go. He breathed out heavily through his noise. "She said her name was Montana."

"Isn't that the name of one of the states? Somewhere in the middle of America?"

"Bordering Canada."

"Is that a real name?"

"For some people. It wasn't her real name."

May knit her brows in thought. "Was she a hooker?"

Ben stared without seeing the ice in his glass. "I wish. It turned out she was a reporter. An undercover reporter."

"What's so bad about that? Was she working on a

story about you and your BDSM proclivities?"

He craned his neck to release a crack. "I don't want to get into the details. Suffice it to say, she might have screwed up Uncle Gordon's chances of being elected mayor."

"How?"

The waitress returned to see if he wanted another kuusu, but he ordered water instead.

"I had suggested Ezra Rosenstein and some other local developers form what's called an I.E., or independent expenditure. In Oakland, there are limits to how much an individual or business can contribute to a candidate, but there are no limits on I.E.s. Ezra agreed to chair the I.E., but he kept communicating with me about it. Kim—Montana got wind of it, and an article was published in the *San Francisco Tribune*."

"What's the big deal?"

"It's against the rules for an I.E. to coordinate with a candidate's campaign. Because of that article, the state is investigating Uncle Gordon for collusion."

Ben cursed himself. If he had been more careful, if he hadn't let his cock do the thinking—or lack thereof—none of this might have come to pass. He had figured out early on that something was up with Kimani. He had been given ample clues in the beginning, and even when he knew she hadn't participated in the Scarlet Auction because she was hard up for money, as she had claimed, he'd ignored all the warning signs. His drive to be with her, to share with her all that he could do to her, overrode his better judgment.

As angry as he was at Kimani, he was angrier at himself.

"I fucked up," he muttered.

May had been silent in thought. "That still doesn't explain why you won't say her name. Her *real* name."

Going over everything that had happened with Kimani had agitated him, and he wondered if Yuki was still around. Or maybe his security detail, Bataar, would be willing to spar with him despite the late hour.

"Because women *meddle*," Ben retorted. "They like to play matchmaker and shit like that."

"Fine. I won't deny I'm curious to look up who she is; who's this slut that got under my brother's skin."

"Anyone who tries to fuck over our family would get under my skin."

"Yeah, but you've come across dozens of people like that. Remember Cousin Chang? He stole twelve million dollars from the Lee Corporation. You weren't as pissed about that."

"That's just money. Uncle Gordon deserves to be mayor."

"But you said people had to pressure him to throw his name in the hat. So running for mayor wasn't something that Uncle was dying to do."

Gordon had told Ben that he could return contentedly to his existing job if he lost.

"It doesn't matter how it started," Ben said. "Uncle Gordon is giving it his all. Without doubt, he's the best candidate for the job. It would benefit everyone if he won."

"Not to mention the Lee Corporation and our waterfront development there. Speaking of which, I thought you wanted to head that up because Uncle was running for mayor."

Ben stiffened. That had been the primary reason for his stay in San Francisco. That, and to recruit an American baller to play for the Golden Phoenix, the Chinese Basketball Association team sponsored by his father. He had returned empty-handed on that front.

"Stone in our San Francisco office is the project manager. He can get the job done."

"Well, that was always the case, wasn't it? You opted to be the lead. Now you're opting out."

"Because I'm a liability."

"And this Montana has nothing to do with that decision?"

Why couldn't women leave well enough alone? He had provided a reasonable explanation, based on business and political practicalities, but a woman had to assume there was more going on.

He jerked his head in the direction of one of the dancers in the cage nearest to May. "She looks like your type."

May looked over. "She's cute, but I heard she's a total *Iero kyabu*."

A *Iero kyabu*, supposedly a reference to the ease with which yellow cabs in New York could be hailed, was someone who allowed herself to get picked up by foreigners.

"Now about this Montana..." May said.

At first Ben was glad to hear his mobile ring, but upon seeing the name displayed on it, he frowned. It was Phyllis. Thanks to his conversation with May, he was in no mood to talk to his older sister and decided to let the call go to voicemail.

Half a minute later, May's mobile rang.

"If it's—" Ben began.

But May had already answered, "Yes, he's here."

May handed him her mobile, which Ben received with his lips pressed grimly in a line.

"She said she needed to talk, like it was urgent," May explained.

"It's nice to know you're avoiding me," Phyllis said through the phone.

"I didn't think it was a good time to talk, given the sort of club I'm at right now," Ben replied. Phyllis had a vague idea of the sort of establishments Ben visited. Knowing that it was sometimes on behalf of business clients, she looked the other way even though she didn't approve.

"Oh."

He could her the frown in her tone.

"Well, we can make this quick," she said. "You want to tell me more about this latest acquisition?"

"No."

"*Huài dàn*," she cursed. "I'm the CFO. You can't just go around acquiring random business without bringing me into it."

"I don't go around acquiring random business," he said.

"Then what is this?"

"An acquisition, but hardly random."

"How is this *San Francisco Tribute*, a newspaper, not random? What are we going to do with a newspaper? Nowhere in the business plan is there an expansion into media, especially with a company that has posted losses for six consecutive quarters. This makes no sense. Based on what I saw of their financials, there's no way you can turn this business around and make a profit."

"I'm not planning to turn them around," Ben replied evenly. "I'm shutting them down."

Chapter Three

"Don't you think it's from that guy Jake?" Sam asked when Kimani showed him the letter the following day.

"It's possible," Kimani acknowledged as she put the letter away in her desk. "Claire wasn't too happy that she didn't get paid by the Scarlet Auction because she didn't complete her week with Jake, but it doesn't seem like something she would do. At least she got an emerald ring out of the whole thing, provided Jake didn't ask for it back. But I don't think the other women got anything."

Somehow, Lisa, the auction participant won by Ben's cousin, Jason, didn't strike her as the type of person who would send threatening notes. Kimani would have bet on Ryan, the anti-feminist won by Jake's buddy, Derek, over Lisa...but Jake was still the most likely culprit. He hated her for sure. She had seen it flaring in his eyes several times, not only when he had thrown her to the floor of his cabin.

"Are you in touch with the other women?"

"I only have Claire's number. Lisa and Ryan don't want to have anything to do with me."

"Jake's the guy who pulled a gun, and they're upset at *you*?"

"They don't get paid unless they fulfill the terms

of the contract in its entirety. I'm the reason their week got cut short."

Sam shook his head. "I don't understand women. Remember Martha in human resources? She caught her husband cheating with a friend of hers, and the only person she blamed was the other woman. Thank God I knew I was gay early in life."

Kimani chuckled despite the unease she had felt ever since receiving the letter. Not wanting to alarm Marissa, she hadn't shared the letter, but she'd had trouble sleeping last night.

"You should show the letter to the police," Sam said.

"And what would they do with it?" Kimani asked. "I'm sure they've got more important matters to handle than figuring out who sent a nasty letter. And all they can do at this point is tell the sender to stop being a bully and writing letters."

"It's too bad Jake posted bail. The guy sounds like he belongs behind bars."

At that moment, the phone on her desk rang. Seeing the number was from the Trinity County District Attorney's Office, she quickly picked up.

"Kimani," said the female assistant district attorney, "how are you holding up?"

"Aside from getting a nasty letter at my house yesterday, I'm okay."

"Oh. Was it from Jake?"

"I'm guessing. Are you calling about him?"

"Yes, and there's no easy way to say this, but the

D.A. has reached a plea deal with Jake."

Kimani frowned. "A plea deal?"

"After talking with you and all the other witnesses, there just isn't enough evidence to prove malicious intent."

"Seriously?"

"He claims he was protecting himself and his home from Mr. Lee and Mr. Lee's bodyguard, whom he called a thug. And given that Mr. Benjamin Lee broke Mr. Vince Donato's arm, it would seem he had cause for fear. The gun was intended for self-defense."

Kimani's mind reeled. "But he punched me in the face!"

"And that qualifies as a simple assault, which is a misdemeanor and carries a penalty of up to one thousand dollars or up to six months in prison. If the judge accepts the plea deal, Jake will pay a thousand dollars."

"What about jail time?"

"He won't serve any."

"A thousand dollars is nothing for a guy like him."

"I'm sorry. The D.A. felt like this was the best way to go. Otherwise, we're looking at having to explain the aspects of, you know, BDSM and when the application of pain qualifies as desired versus unwanted, what you and everyone consented to. It just gets really muddy."

"So that's it?"

"I'm sorry, Kimani. Not to diminish what you suffered, but our jails would be bursting at the seams if we locked up every idiot who threw a punch. Last year, my seven-year-old gave another kid a bloody nose on the school playground. My son won't ever be doing that again, and I'm sure Jake has learned his lesson."

Has he? Kimani questioned internally.

"Bad news?" Sam asked after Kimani had hung up.

"Jake and the D.A.'s office reached a plea deal. He's going to pay a fine but serve no time."

"You could try a civil suit. Sue him for emotional distress."

Kimani shook her head and grabbed her handbag. "Not worth it. I'm okay. He's not the only asshole in this world. And maybe he'll clean up his act now."

She hoped it was true, but deep down, she didn't believe it.

*****

"Mr. Lee, thank you for meeting with me," Kimani said as she took a seat opposite Ben's uncle in the small office of his campaign headquarters, located in an old warehouse that used to house a dance studio. Outside the glass walls of his office, volunteers busily bundled literature pieces, stamped letters, and assembled lawn signs.

Gordon returned a warm smile. Either he didn't recognize her as the young woman Ben had brought to lunch with him to the soul food restaurant, or Ben hadn't told him the part she'd played in sparking the FPPC investigation.

"It's Montana, right?"

"Actually, it's Kimani Taylor," she corrected a little sheepishly.

"My apologies. I'm usually better with names."

She didn't feel right letting him think the error was this. "I let Ben introduce me as Montana the time we had lunch at Maybelle's. Kimani's my real name."

A brief look of puzzlement crossed his round face, but he didn't pry. "What can I do for you, Kimani?"

She took in a deep breath. If Ben hadn't told his uncle—she wasn't sure why he wouldn't have—she needed to come clean and get it off her conscience.

"I work for the *San Francisco Tribune*," she blurted, then waited for his reaction.

"Ah." His brows knit briefly in thought. "That's a very good paper. I hope they're able to continue their good work for years to come."

She blinked several times, surprised by the sincerity in his tone. He didn't harbor any ill will towards the paper that may have hurt his chances of winning the election?

"You're not upset, Mr. Lee?"

"Please, call me Gordon. What is there to be upset about?"

"The *Tribune* ran an article about Oakland Forward, and now you're being investigated by the FPPC."

He gave her a sympathetic smile even though he was the one who deserved the sympathy. "I won't say it didn't hurt. But my campaign has done nothing wrong, and the investigation will show that."

"But I saw you dropped several points in the most recent polling Channel 2 did on the race."

"We'll make it back up."

She perked up. "I think I can help—in a way. The *Tribune* wants to do a profile of you, and all the other candidates, of course. I think it will help the voters get to know you better, on a personal level. It'll be more interesting than the campaign literature they receive in their mail."

"Well, I am honored. I don't know that I'm that interesting."

"Your background is very interesting: how you came to this country and worked two jobs as a high school student to support yourself even though your family could probably afford to buy an entire college; all the work you did as a nonprofit housing attorney—the pro bono cases you took on behalf of tenants who couldn't afford a lawyer; the role you played in securing a location for mental health services in Chinatown."

"That was a team effort."

"From what I heard, you were the one who actually made it all happen, but you let Councilwoman Huang take the credit."

"It's not important who gets the credit."

"See, that's exactly what the voters don't see but should—your modesty, your dedication to improving the community. Right now, a lot of voters think you're just a puppet for business interests. And Oakland

Forward reinforces that perception." She paused and decided to rush the words out before they stuck in her throat. "And it's my fault."

"Your fault?"

"When I was, um, spending time with Ben, I saw a text from Ezra Rosenstein to your nephew. I told my editor about it."

He made no response, so she continued.

"I'm sorry. It was a private text, and I...I'm sorry."

"Well, there was nothing untrue in that article."

"Ben didn't, um, say anything to you about it?"

"He blamed himself for the article and acknowledged that Oakland Forward had been his idea initially. I would have told him a PAC was unnecessary, but it is what it is. Did Ben know you worked for the *Tribune*?"

"Technically, I wasn't with the paper at the time I knew Ben, and I never told him I was a reporter. How... How is Ben?"

"I haven't heard from him recently. I think he's in Tokyo right now."

"He didn't do anything wrong. I believe he was trying to do everything right. And he's completely devoted to you and your campaign. I...I misled him, and because of that, you're being investigated by the FPPC." She bit her lower lip. "I wouldn't blame you if you—and Ben—hated me."

"I can't speak for Ben, but hate doesn't do anyone any good."

"Will you still let the *Tribune* do a profile? I don't

have to be the reporter writing it."

A woman knocked and opened the door. "Gordon, your precinct folder for East Oakland is ready."

"Thank you," Gordon replied to her.

"You're walking East Oakland?" Kimani asked him.

"Why not?"

"Not a lot of people choose to walk East Oakland."

"I don't feel right ignoring the neighborhoods there just because they're not the safest."

"If you're still good with the *Tribune* doing a profile, I'd love to have one of our reporters and a cameraman join you on your walk."

"Sure. Will you be coming along as well?"

"Only if you don't mind."

"I would be happy for you to come," he said with a forgiving smile.

Her emotions swelled. Her instincts on Gordon had been right. She only wished her instincts had been right about Ben. Or maybe they *had* been right—she just hadn't listened to them.

She had no expectations that Gordon would tell Ben that she'd apologized, but if Gordon could forgive her, maybe one day Ben could as well.

Chapter Four

In his dreams, Ben ravished her against the walls of the caves located on the beaches of one of the Lee Corporation's resorts in Thailand. Or he fucked her hard and rough while she struggled in rope bondage—hogtie, frogtie, strappado, piledriver—he'd do them all with her. It didn't matter that she wasn't the experience sub she'd pretended to be for the Scarlet Auction.

And sometimes they made love beneath a cloudless California sky.

Whatever the dream, Ben always woke to the most annoying hard-on. He had banged plenty of women since leaving San Francisco, but it felt like he was suffering from blue balls. All because he couldn't fuck *her*.

"It's stabilized," his pollster had called to tell him. "I think Gordon's taken all the hit there is from the FPPC investigation—unless something new comes out."

"You think the *Tribune* is still digging?" asked Ben as he stood fully dressed in a suit and looked out the window of his hotel room at the Tokyo skyline. Turning around, he looked to his bed, where two naked women lay. One of them had woken up and started to pet the breasts of the other.

Ben had jacked off in the shower earlier instead of waking the women.

"I have no idea, but their readership in Oakland has shrunk a lot in recent years, so their impact is limited. The question is whether or not the other news outlets will pick up on the story, too."

The *Tribune's readership will be zero soon enough*, Ben thought to himself. He'd had his attorney, Murray Jones, form an LLC to facilitate the purchase of the *Tribune* so it wouldn't be immediately traceable to the Lee family. He didn't want any negative press to come from it.

The two women were now kissing. Having concluded his call with his pollster, Ben took a few minutes to watch the women, their soft white limbs wrapped around each other.

"You know she works there now," Stephens, who handled special projects and had done the initial research on Kimani, had told him when Ben had first sat down with him to discuss shutting down the *Tribune*.

Ben had narrowed his eyes, suspecting he knew whom Stephens referred to. "Who?"

"Kimani Taylor. The woman you had me look up. She started there a few days ago."

"You mean she wasn't with the paper when... She wasn't there before?"

"Not on the payroll. She was working for some finance firm."

It hadn't mattered whether Kimani was formally

with the paper or not. She had been doing her job as a reporter.

"So she'll be out of a job," Bataar had said.

Ben had given the large Mongolian a hard look. "Not my problem."

Kimani was smart, Ben had reasoned. She would land on her feet. Maybe she wouldn't have the job she wanted, but she was too capable to starve.

Still, he felt a stab of guilt. And anger. He shouldn't feel guilty over a woman who had played fast and loose with his family's affairs.

The women on his bed were now kissing each other vigorously. One started masturbating the other, who made soft lilting pants. Remembering how delicious each gasp and every groan of Kimani's had sounded, he felt a faint stirring in his crotch.

Not every memory of Kimani had to do with sex. He remembered how stunning she had looked for their dinner at Ishikawa West in that halter and her new weave. He remembered how her face had lit up the first time she had gotten up on her water-skis, the gleam in her eyes as they played one-on-one basketball outside on the patio of his penthouse, the way her brow furrowed when he'd made her drink hot tea on a summer day, the passion in her voice when she talked about social issues.

He remembered everything.

A knock sounded at the door. Bataar was here to drive him to his meeting with investors.

After adjusting himself and taking one last look at

the women, who had now angled themselves with legs spread wide so they could grind their genitalia against each other, Ben went to get the door.

"Morning, boss," Bataar greeted, his gaze going over Ben's shoulder to the bed.

"Want a minute?" Ben offered, turning so that Bataar could have a less obstructed view.

Bataar shook his head. "Too early in the morning. I don't want to have to battle a hard-on for the rest of the day."

With a laugh, Ben closed the door behind him and the two men headed to the elevator. Once inside, Bataar shared some news that did not please Ben.

"Stephens told me it's official—Jake pled out on misdemeanor charges."

Ben frowned. "Bastard."

"Yeah. His bodyguard, too. Total pussy underneath that tough-guy exterior."

"I was referring to the district attorney for not pinning Jake with something more than a misdemeanor."

"I guess if he tried Jake for aggravated assault, he'd have to try you as well. I'm surprised Vince didn't press charges for his broken arm."

"He still could. I doubt the statute of limitations has run out."

"Probably doesn't want it publicly known that he got beat up."

Ben didn't care one way or another if Vince wanted to press charges against him, except that it might generate negative publicity for Gordon, who probably couldn't afford to get hit with any more scandal, even though it involved extended family and not the candidate himself.

"I put a guy on Jake ever since he made bail," Bataar said as they stepped out of the elevator. "I just don't trust the fucker."

Ben clenched his jaw. Kimani had been right about Jake all along. He should have listened to her. Instead, he had actually considered handing her back to the son of a bitch. If he hadn't returned to the cabin when he had...

He cursed himself.

"According to my guy, Chin Ko, Jake went by her place."

Ben stopped and turned swiftly to stare at Bataar. "What do you mean?"

"He didn't go in or try to talk to her."

"By 'her,' you mean Kimani."

"Of course, boss. She's the one you're interested in."

Ben was about to tell Bataar to keep his personal observations to himself, but he wanted to hear what else he had to say about Jake.

"Chin said Jake parked his car across from her duplex and sat there for ten minutes before driving away."

What the fuck...

"Anything else unusual?"

"Not so far. I've got Stephens' hacker in Singapore

trying to track Jake's movements online, but we haven't hit on anything yet."

Ben felt a pit in his stomach. "Put a guy on Kimani."

"Twenty-four seven?"

"Of course. Why do a job half-assed?"

"I'm going to need a bigger budget."

"You already went over budget when you hired Chin."

"Just want to be sure, boss."

His blood pressure soaring, Ben started walking again. Bataar had to scramble to keep up. Once outside, Ben put on his shades, the same pair of Louis Vuitton that he'd lent to Kimani their first day on Jake's boat.

Ben's car was waiting out front. After he and Bataar got in, Ben turned to the man who had watched out for him for the better part of seven years. "If anything happens to her, you're fired."

Bataar had a look of self-satisfaction on his wide mug. "Anything else, boss?"

Ben frowned. "Yeah. I'll fuck you up so bad, your dick will be coming out your nose."

Seeing that his boss wasn't joking, Bataar only nodded. "Okay, boss."

Chapter Five

"That was fun," said Robin Alvarez, a fellow reporter at the *Tribune*, after they had returned to the campaign headquarters for Gordon Lee. "I've never been on a precinct walk before."

She turned to Ron, the bearded photographer for the paper. "Did you get any good pics?"

Ron was scrolling through the photos he had taken of Gordon. "Yeah, I got some good action shots. Check these out."

Kimani and Robin peered over his shoulder as he scrolled through pictures of Gordon talking to voters, Gordon wiping his brow as the Indian summer sun beat down on him during the second hour of their precinct walk. Gordon cheerfully waving to passersby, and Gordon laughing after he missed a terrible shot on a basketball court.

"I like that one," Kimani said when Ron landed on a photo of Gordon taking a break, sitting down on the sidewalk with a stack of his campaign literature next to him, a wall of graffiti behind him. Gordon had remarked at the time that he wanted to look into supporting the expansion of mural projects for East Oakland.

"This is going to be a great piece," said Robin. "I

can't wait to write it. I mean, cowrite this with you, Kimani."

"It's all yours," Kimani said. "I'll help you with the research, but I don't need to be in the byline."

Robin and Ron looked at her in disbelief.

"But you're the one who set up the interview with Gordon," Robin said.

"He would've said yes if you had asked. It's better if I..." She decided not to finish her thought, in case it raised questions with Robin and Ron. "You're the more experienced writer, anyway."

"Yeah, but you're new. Don't you want to get every byline you can?"

Kimani looked at the tables where precinct maps, voter lists, and door hangers had been organized by neighborhoods. The neighborhood with the largest stacks of folders and literature was East Oakland.

"I shouldn't have the byline because I'm biased," Kimani explained. "This way, I can volunteer for Gordon's campaign."

"I have to admit, he doesn't come across as much of a dynamic leader," Ron, who lived in Oakland, said, "but I'd definitely consider voting for him now. He's seems to know his stuff."

"I'll see you back at the office," Kimani said, "I'm going to take my lunch break here in Oakland."

She grabbed a folder and some door hangers from the East Oakland pile.

"I'll take this precinct," she told the coordinator in charge of precinct walking.

The young woman took a look at the precinct map. "That's East Oakland. I have a few neighborhoods left in the Rockridge area if you want one of those."

"Yeah, but it doesn't look like you have a lot of folks walking East Oakland."

"Well, they're not the safest neighborhoods, especially for women. You're not planning to walk the precinct alone?"

"I grew up in Oakland. I know my way around."

"Still, I don't think Gordon would be okay with that. If anyone on the campaign were to get hurt—"

"I just came back from walking an East Oakland precinct with Gordon."

"Still, I'd feel better if you took one of the other neighborhoods. Even this one off International Boulevard is better."

"Okay," Kim relented. She accepted the new packet from the coordinator.

But on her way out, when no one was looking, she grabbed an East Oakland packet.

*****

She took an hour lunch break to drop door hangers in East Oakland before taking the BART, Bay Area Rapid Transit, train back into the city. When she arrived at the *Tribune* offices, she sensed something wrong the instant she walked into the newsroom.

Robin rushed up to her. "You missed the big announcement," she said.

At first, Kim thought it was the good news that Sam had hinted at the other day, but the air of despair didn't match her expectation.

"What was the big announcement?" Kim asked.

"We've all been given two weeks' notice."

After a moment of stunned silence, Kim asked, "They're shutting down the paper?"

"I guess we all saw it coming, but I thought we'd hear about it with more notice than two weeks."

Kim went to find Sam, who was sitting in his office looking out the window.

"I missed the announcement. We've all been given two weeks' notice?"

Sam swiveled around, a resigned look on his face. "I'm afraid so. I'm sorry your job here didn't last very long."

"So it's definite? I thought there was a chance the paper would stay open with new ownership."

"I thought so, too. Why else would anyone want to acquire us?"

"Who's the new owner?"

"Some company called New Western Media. I've never heard of them. Turns out they're newly formed. Their paperwork was filed recently with the Secretary of State's office."

Kimani sank down into a nearby chair. "New Western Media. Do you think they're affiliated with a rival paper?"

"I wondered that at first, but we know all the owners of the various media outlets in this geographic area. New Western Media doesn't seem to be linked to any of them. The only good news in this is that we all get a severance package worth three months' salary and extended health insurance."

Her jaw dropped. "Three months! That's very generous. And odd."

"I thought so, too. I quizzed Ralph, one of the original owners. He said he was just as stunned about the closure. He actually thought New Western Media was a good Samaritan, an angel funder, who was coming in to save the paper. It's the strangest thing. This company acquires us in record time, all shrouded in mystery, and the only communication we get from our new owners is a letter from their attorney's office providing the two weeks' notice and details of the severance package."

"Do we at least get to keep the press going during our last two weeks?"

"I think so. There was no mention of turning off the presses immediately."

"So, will we still have time to run the profiles of the mayoral candidates?"

"If you hustle."

She nodded. "I'll get it done."

"When you start job hunting, I'm happy to be a reference for you. Just know that I'll be serving as a reference for many of your colleagues as well. I hope everyone lands something."

"What about you?"

"I guess I could always be a lecturer again. I like

teaching, but I'll miss the press. I'll miss the clicking and clacking of computer keys in the newsroom. I'll miss hunting down a good story."

"What should we do about the Scarlet Auction scoop?"

"Has the district attorney given you any indication when they'll be wrapping up their investigation?"

She shook her head.

"Call them and ask. I'd like to honor their request, but circumstances have changed."

"Will do."

Sam swiveled his chair back around to stare out his office window. She felt bad for him. And hoped that he would find a new job situation to his liking soon.

The rest of the afternoon moved slowly, with many of the *Tribune* staff still in shock.

"Maybe I'll have to be a wedding photographer for a while," Ron said.

With only two weeks to work on the mayoral candidate profiles, Kimani worked at a faster pace assembling the background research. By the time she looked up at the clock, it was past nine o'clock. After hopping on the light rail back to her place, she arrived home at ten o'clock. As she walked up to the duplex, she noticed that the lights were on.

Marissa was supposed to work the last shift at the bar and grill tonight, so had her roommate come home early?

Kimani walked up to the front door—and saw it

was slightly ajar. That was strange. Marissa didn't usually leave the door open, but maybe she had forgotten something and was planning to head out the door again.

Suddenly, Kimani couldn't shake the feeling that she was being watched again. Turning her head, she looked behind and scanned the streets, sidewalk and other homes. Except for a car passing by several blocks down, it was quiet. No one happened to be out at the moment. Kimani would have felt comfort in even the sound of crickets, but there were none.

She pushed the door open a little. "Marissa?"

Instead of a verbal reply, a thud made Kimani jump. . For some reason, she couldn't bring herself to go in. If it wasn't Marissa, maybe it was their landlords? But they had never come unannounced, and they were supposed to be on a Caribbean cruise.

"Marissa!" she tried again.

This time her heart stalled completely when a man dressed in black, a ski mask over his face, appeared in the doorway.

"Well, if it isn't the reporter," he sneered.

She thought of screaming, but the man grabbed her arm, stalling her intended response.

Just then, the sound of a loud, persistent cough came from across the street.

The intruder's eyes widened behind his ski mask. Releasing her, he bolted past Kimani. He had something tucked beneath his arm as he ran around three houses, turned the block, and was out of sight.

The man across the street continued to have a coughing fit.

Though still rattled, Kimani ran over to the man. "You want me to get you a glass of water?"

He waved his hand and shook his head. His coughing subsided. "I'm fine. Thanks."

He then went on his way. She didn't recognize him as someone who lived on their block, but there was a handful of apartments in the neighborhood, so she couldn't know everyone.

He had seemed to come out of nowhere. She was sure she hadn't seen anyone for blocks, but she was immensely grateful that he happened to be walking by.

Pulling out her cellphone, she called the police. She wasn't going to go inside on the chance that the intruder had a buddy, even though that prospect hadn't crossed her mind when she'd offered the coughing man water.

She called Marissa next.

"Yeah, I'm still at work," her roommate replied. "The bar and grill closes at eleven. Why?"

"Someone broke into our place. The police are on their way."

"Oh my God! I want to be there. It's slow enough at work, I'm sure I can leave early."

"Okay, see you soon."

Still feeling like she was being watched—maybe the intruder was lurking about—Kimani didn't feel safe waiting on the streets by herself and decided to knock on a neighbor's door. Mrs. Sanchez and her elderly mother went to bed early, so it took a while for her to come to the door. She let Kimani stay in her house while she waited for the police to arrive.

"*Dios mio*," Mrs. Sanchez murmured with a brow furrowed in worry. She had a bolt and a chain lock on her door. Kimani wondered if she would be installing extra protection on her own door soon. "And I thought this was a relatively safe neighborhood. I did consider moving out of the city before, but Mama's not interested in the suburbs. Says only white-washed Latinos live in the suburbs."

Kimani managed to smile and even consume a pupusa that Mrs. Sanchez insisted on warming up for her.

After two police officers arrived and went inside and deemed the premises safe, Kimani was allowed to enter her home.

The place had been turned upside down. Every drawer was open, their contents strewn all over the floor. In her bedroom, her clothes covered her bed and floor. Even the clothes hanging in her closet had been ripped out.

"So what was taken?" an Officer Nguyen asked.

"My laptop," she replied, seeing the bare spot on her desk. That was what the intruder had been carrying under his arm.

"What else?"

"That's it, I think."

"What about jewelry?"

Kimani looked at the earrings and necklaces

hanging out of her jewelry box. "I don't own any jewelry worth stealing, but it looks like it's all here."

The other officer walked up. "The TV looks untouched, along with the wifi router and Blu-ray disc player. You must have interrupted the thief before he could grab much."

"I don't think it was a thief," she replied. Walking over to Marissa's room and seeing it in order—relative order, as Marissa tended to let her laundry lie about her room—confirmed her suspicion. "The guy knew I was a reporter."

"He said something to you?"

"Something along the lines of, 'well, it's the reporter.'"

"Did the guy say anything else?"

She shook her head.

"We've seen an uptick in the number of threats to journalists in the past few years. Which news outlet do you work for?"

The officers asked her several more questions, including whether or not the *Tribune* had received any threats. They also asked her for a description of the intruder. When Marissa arrived shortly after, they questioned her as well.

"It does seem like a guy was targeting you," Officer Nguyen said to Kimani. "We could dust for prints, but if you're pretty certain he was wearing gloves, we won't waste our time."

"He was covered from head to toe," she replied. Only the little bit of skin she had seen through the eyeholes of the ski mask had clued her in that the intruder was likely white, possibly Latino.

After the police officers left, Kim turned to a visibly shaken Marissa. "I'll see if I can go in to work late tomorrow and clean everything up. You okay?"

"I'm wishing I hadn't given up smoking," Marissa said with a nervous laugh. "Is it reasonable that I'm, like, totally freaked out?"

"I'm freaked out, too."

"I almost want to go to The Lair. I need something to calm me down, and the wine cooler in the fridge isn't going to cut it."

"Is The Lair open at this time of night?"

"It's open till two in the morning. You never know when you might need a late night flogging. You should come."

Kim stiffened. The only person who had ever flogged her was Ben. She couldn't imagine receiving a flogging from anyone else, especially a stranger.

"It's a lot healthier than smoking or drinking," Marissa coaxed.

"Thanks for the invite, but I want to at least put all my clothes back in their drawers. Maybe next time."

Marissa raised her brows. "That's the first time you've been receptive to going to The Lair. I'm gonna hold you to it."

Kimani hesitated, but going to a BDSM club with Marissa was the least of her worries. She hadn't wanted to worry Marissa about the note, but she had to believe that and the break-in were connected. What would

Jake want with her laptop? Was he worried that she had incriminating photos of him? But he had to know anything she had, like the recordings she had on her pens, would have been turned over to the District Attorney's Office.

Maybe he broke in to her home just to harass her? At first she had considered that the intruder himself was Jake, but the former was too thin. And it fit that Jake would have someone else do the dirty work for him. A judge had also placed a restraining order on him. He wasn't supposed to go within a hundred feet of her.

Recalling the grip on her arm by the intruder, Kimani shuddered. She was sure he had intended to pull her into the house, but she didn't want to think about what he might have done after that. She made a mental note to buy one of the bolt locks Mrs. Sanchez had on her door.

Chapter Six

"*Uhsnei Hiej*," swore Bataar, holding the side of his face where Ben's fist had landed. Somehow Ben had felled the large man. "What was that for?"

Ignoring the gasps and gawks from people passing by them on the sidewalk and a woman telling her husband to call the police, Ben stared at the head of his security detail. "You're fired. I'll let you throw the next punch, but then you're getting your arse kicked."

"She wasn't hurt," Bataar insisted. "My guy was there. Moe prevented anything more from happening."

Ben drew in a breath to lower his blood pressure as he took in what Bataar said.

"And he stuck around the rest of the night to make sure the guy didn't return," Bataar continued. "I've got the new guy, Bill, on the next shift, so she's covered twenty-four hours a day."

Ben took in another long breath. The rational side of him advised against firing Bataar, as he was unlikely to find a more loyal and effective bodyguard, someone willing to take a kick to the head whenever his employer wanted to blow off steam, but his anger wanted a punching bag at the moment.

Someone had broken into her residence. Luckily that's all that had happened. So far.

Fuck. It meant he couldn't put Kimani behind him, no matter how much he wanted to shove her into the past and have her stay there.

"Was it Jake?" Ben asked.

"Chin was with Jake. The guy spent the night at some woman's place."

"Doesn't mean Jake wasn't behind it."

Bataar got to his feet and nodded. "I know."

"Did this Moe catch the guy in her house? Did he see what he looked like?"

"If Moe had tried, he would have exposed himself. He decided his priority was making sure Kimani didn't get hurt. I've got someone trying to hack into the SFPD to pull up the report. Maybe Kimani noticed something and told the cops."

Feeling his anger recede, Ben started to walk, his mind turning. The gawkers stared in puzzlement as Bataar hurried alongside him as if nothing had happened.

"I want *you* on Kimani," Ben said after a few minutes. "Not some new untested guy."

"Bill worked for the Secret Service. FLOTUS detail. I don't think we're going to find anyone better."

"Don't give me excuses."

"You're my charge. That hasn't changed in over seven years."

"It's changing today."

"Look, I know you're worried about her because—"

Ben stopped and turned to Bataar. "You want me

to aim for your nose this time?"

"I've had my nose broken three times. You're welcome to make it four, boss."

Ben's hand curled into a fist, but he couldn't punch Bataar just for the hell of it. Sparring was one thing, but breaking Bataar's nose wouldn't serve a purpose. He uncurled his hand.

"It's not optimal for me to shadow her, especially without her spotting me," Bataar explained. "I'm a big Mongolian. Even here in Japan and China, I stick out. Bill's a white guy. He can move about without notice much better."

Bataar returned Ben's stare for a few seconds before adding, "If anything happens to her, I'll save you the trouble and beat the shit out of myself."

Ben released his breath. They walked in silence back to the hotel. If Bataar had been a woman, he would probably comment or make inquiries as to what his boss' anger implied about certain feelings for Kimani. While the masculine and feminine both reside in an individual, Bataar had rarely demonstrated the latter quality save in his mother bear protection of Ben. Although privy to all of Ben's personal affairs, Bataar had always kept his nose out. He was a sparring partner, not a drinking buddy. He never tried to be anything but the head of Ben's security detail, not even a friend.

Ben decided to chalk Bataar's uncharacteristic toe-dipping into the arena of *feelings* to the motive of giving Ben a hard time just for the hell of it—a normal masculine activity. If Ben didn't have the tolerance for talking about Kimani with May, his confidante since they were children, he sure as hell wasn't going to talk about her with Bataar.

If asked, he would admit that Kimani had been fun to hang out with, fun to fuck. Her arse was sweeter than eight-treasure rice. And he should have helped himself to more of it when he'd had the chance. He also felt responsible for her. He had taken her off Jake's hands, had become her Master. If he hadn't ticked Jake off so much, Jake might not have taken his aggression out on her because he was too much the pussy to confront the true source of his insecurity.

It all might have turned out better if he had never bought her in the first place. He wouldn't bet high on that, but what was supposed to have been just a week of harmless sex had turned into a messy complication involving depositions with the Trinity County District Attorney's office and an earful from his cousin Jason's father, who had charged Ben with looking after Jason.

"According to our attorney, Jason has nothing to worry about," Ben had told his uncle.

"The fact that we need an attorney in the first place is unacceptable," Jason's father had responded.

Ben couldn't dispute that. He had failed to keep Jason away from trouble. It didn't matter that Jake had been Jason's friend to begin with or that Ben had initially opted out of the Scarlet Auction. Everything got fucked up because he had to have Kimani.

Back at the hotel, Ben decided that swimming laps

in the pool might help calm his agitation. Even though he had decided he didn't like Kimani—not after what she had done—he didn't want her to come to any harm as a result of his spat with Jake. He didn't want that on his conscience.

Looking forward to his swim, Ben was taken aback to find his hotel room occupied. Not by the hotel maids or the twins, whom he had bid goodbye to in the morning, but by a slender woman in a hip-hugging scarlet dress. Even sitting down on his bed, she looked all legs. Standing, she would be six-feet tall. Her baps were larger than the last time Ben had seen her, so she must have gotten a second augmentation. Her long black curls were styled like some actress from the Golden Age of Hollywood, a skinny Chinese version of Rita Hayworth.

"Eumie," he greeted, unsurprised that she had gotten access to his hotel room. Women of her beauty—she was aptly named Eu-meh, which meant "especially beautiful"—could get almost anything. He was surprised that she knew he was in Tokyo.

"I bumped into May in the hotel lobby," Eumie Ma explained. "I'm staying here, too."

"What brings you to Tokyo?" Ben asked of his ex-girlfriend. She was one of the reasons he had decided that, unless it had to do with family or business, sex was all he wanted from women at the moment.

"Doing a photo shoot for a new fashion designer. What about you?"

"Business," he replied simply. Eumie didn't have

much of an interest in anything outside of fashion and gossip. Kimani would have inquired into what kind of business, and he would have been happy to indulge all her questions about the intricacies of real estate development.

He took off his jacket and hung it up in the closet. He still intended to go swimming. It didn't matter that a runway model might be interested in something else.

They were different in other ways, too. Eumie would never want to shoot hoops or play ball of any kind for fear of breaking a nail. Ben would not have been surprised if she had never picked up a ball in her entire life. And while she enjoyed naughty sex, she had never allowed him to use a flogger or any impact toy on her because she needed her skin unblemished for her swimsuit photos.

"Your sister said you're in town till the end of the week. So am I."

He undid the top buttons of his shirt and pulled it over head. She gave a small grunt as her gaze traveled over his pectorals and six-pack.

"Maybe we can have drinks later," he said.

Her cherry-red lips curled downward, but he could tell she wasn't giving up yet. She crossed one leg over the other, causing her short dress to ride up a little farther. He remembered exactly what her pussy looked like, with its soft white folds, always smooth because she kept up with her Brazilian bikini waxes. Warmth began to stir in his groin. But he continued to undress, unbuckling his belt and pulling off his pants so that he stood only in his briefs.

"It looks like you're not off to a meeting," she said. "And I'm done for the day, so..."

He grabbed his swim trunks from the dresser. "I was going to go for a swim."

He stopped short of inviting her to join him.

"That sounds fun. Maybe I'll join you after..."

"After what?"

Sliding off the bed, she stood up and ambled toward him. The potency of her perfume overwhelmed him. He had smelled it the instant he'd opened the door. Now that she was inches from him, it burned his nose. Why did some women douse themselves with this shit as if they had lost their sense of smell?

He bet Kimani understood moderation. In fact, he didn't remember her wearing any perfume during their time together. And she still smelled good. Especially when she was aroused.

His cock throbbed just as Eumie trailed a finger down his left pec.

"You know we haven't seen each other in over a year," she said.

"What happened to your British movie star?" he asked of her latest boyfriend.

"He got a little too possessive for me."

Ben didn't point out the irony of her statement. Eumie tended toward jealousy, and her insecurity—texting him every other hour if he was abroad and eying every woman with suspicion—had been the downfall of their short-lived relationship. Admittedly, he hadn't done his best to allay her worst fears, but he didn't have the time and temperament to coddle her.

"So here we are, both of us single and unattached," she said.

Her finger now scraped his abdomen.

"How do you know I'm unattached?" he replied.

"Well, May thought you might have someone in the United States, but she couldn't say for sure."

Ben would hazard that even if he did have a girlfriend, it wouldn't stop Eumie's advances. He looked down at her enticing cleavage, and his urge to swim waned.

"What are you really trying to say?" he asked as her finger slid over his crotch. His cock hardened.

"I think you know what I'm suggesting."

He returned a look of exasperation. Why did so many women feel the need to be coy? This sort of beating around the bush was a bloody waste of time. Kimani had been less than straightforward. While she hadn't been evasive just for the hell of it—she was doing her job and trying to hide her identity as an undercover reporter—her lack of truthfulness still rankled him.

"Well?" Eumie prompted.

Ben stared at her lips, inches from his. Women liked to play this sort of game—get the man to speak aloud what the woman was thinking.

He cut to the chase. Grabbing her by the back of her neck, he crushed his mouth over hers, smearing her lipstick.

She stiffened in surprise, then went all soft on him. As usual, she allowed him to direct the kissing, perfectly content to be the recipient of the action. Her lips were not as plump as Kimani's, but they possessed the soft suppleness he had come to expect from women. After taking a brief moment to set the tone— he was in charge—he stumbled her back toward the bed. They fell onto it. Eumie purred as he kissed his way down her throat to her décolletage. The mischievous part of him considered giving her a hickey, but knowing that she had a photo shoot and how she would react, he decided it wasn't worth it. He yanked the sleeves down her shoulders to expose more of her breast.

"Hey!" she yelped. "Be careful with my dress. It's a Vera Wang."

Ignoring her—if she really cared that much about the dress, she shouldn't have tried to seduce him—he continued to pull the sleeves down past her pink lace bra. Yanking the bra cup down, he bared her rosy areola.

Kimani had mocha-colored areolas, large areolas that took up almost a third of the breast. His cock stiffened further at the memory.

When he started devouring Eumie's nipple, she seemed to forget about her dress. She wriggled beneath him. "Do you like my new tits?"

"Sure," he replied, squeezing the orb and finding it firm to the touch, not nearly as pliable and soft like real breast tissue.

She arched her back as he continued to suck and bite her nipple.

"If we go through with this," he said, "it's a fuck for fuck's sake. Nothing more."

"You're so romantic, Benji."

"I don't want any misunderstanding."

"A fuck for fuck's sake. That's all I'm looking for."

Satisfied with her response, he reached beneath her dress and rubbed her crotch, feeling the dampness on her lace panties. He remembered how wet he could make Kimani. He remembered making her squirt for her first time. That was much better than popping cherries as Jake liked to do.

Knowing that Eumie liked the attention to her breasts, he went to town on them while he groped her between the legs. She gasped and sighed, and sighed and gasped. He intended for the sex to be relatively quick, not the drawn-out episodes he saved for his subs, and Eumie was aroused enough that she wouldn't need a lot of foreplay. Pulling aside her lace thong, he fondled her clitoris.

"Oh, Benji," she purred, a starry look in her eyes as she gazed at him.

"Missed me, didn't you?" he returned.

She shrugged. "A little."

He sank two digits into her hot, wet snatch, making her moan. "Just a little?"

He worked her till she was panting and writhing.

"Okay, maybe more than a little," she admitted between sharp breaths.

He pulled her panties off and stuffed them between her ruby-red lips. "Taste that? That's more than a little, love."

After fetching a condom, he spread her legs and settled between them. He pulled out his cock and slipped on the condom. Eumie had always been good about taking her birth control pills, but he wasn't going to take any chances

"Nice shave," he commented, noting her bald mound.

Removing the panties from her mouth, she beamed at the compliment as he ran his finger through her hair, thick and straight compared to the delicate curls adorning Kimani's mound.

He aimed his prick at her slit and shoved inside her wet heat. He closed his eyes and saw himself sinking into Kimani. His member throbbed.

With Kimani, he would have lowered himself onto his elbows so that he could take her mouth while he thrust into her. But he stayed upright with Eumie to avoid her perfume. He rolled his hips, driving himself deeper, imagining Kimani's hips grinding in rhythm to his. He would pin her wrists above her head with one hand if they weren't already tied together with his favorite hemp rope. His other hand would grasp her breast and pinch her nipple, lightly if she was being good, hard if she wasn't.

Of course he would pinch her nipple hard. She hadn't been very good at all. She had been very, very bad. She didn't deserve to be made love to. She deserved to be fucked. Punished. Without safety words. Maybe without coming. He'd punish her so fucking hard—

"Benji!"

Realizing that Eumie had called his name twice in succession, and that he had been pounding away more harshly than he'd intended, he stopped. He rolled his hips more gently, searching for the angle that made the eyes roll toward the back of her head. He found a rhythm and depth that made her tighten her hands around his forearms.

"Damn, you're so good," she moaned.

Minutes later, she was convulsing and screaming. He used the moment to thrust harder and quicker, but his release didn't come as soon as expected. Withdrawing, he flipped her onto her stomach before plunging back in. He slapped his pelvis against her creamy white buttocks—and when he pictured himself sinking into Kimani's arse, he erupted.

How many women would he have to fuck before he stopped seeing Kimani in his mind? he wondered as he lay in post-coital haze with Eumie curled beside him.

He thought about the man who had broken into Kimani's place. What the fuck was Jake up to? Could he trust the San Francisco police to figure it out? Or Bataar and the former Secret Service he hired?

Ben wanted answers, and he wanted them now. He wasn't content to just sit and wait for SFPD or Bataar. He didn't like that he was over 5,000 miles away, unable to do shit. And if he could resolve the issue and put his mind at ease, then maybe he could finally be done with her.

He would fly out to San Francisco himself.

Sooner rather than later.

*****

Wrapped in a thick robe, May, who had finished a massage treatment at the hotel spa, stood at the edge of the pool.

"I meant to text you earlier that Eumie is here," she said as Ben got out of the water. "I tried to hint to her that you were interested in someone in California."

Ben toweled off his wet hair. "She didn't take the hint."

"Sorry about that. I tried to spare you."

Ben sat down on a lounge chair and ordered tea from the poolside server, aware that May was eying him keenly.

"Guess it was just as well," May continued. "You fucked her, didn't you?"

May had never been a big fan of Eumie's, possibly because May had hit on Eumie first, and Eumie had not received May's flirtation as a compliment.

Lying back, he closed his eyes. "So what if I did?"

"Don't you remember what she was like?"

"She's not interested in getting back together."

May snorted. "Of course that's what she's going to tell you. She's old school at this game. She knows playing hard to get still works with men."

Ben wondered if Kimani had ever played hard to get. He couldn't see it.

"Maybe she's at the same place as me," he said. "Women aren't always interested in a relationship. You were the one who told me that women are not biologically predisposed to monogamy, that it's a construct men imposed on women to keep them from having too much sex."

May rolled her eyes. "But, deep down, Eumie's old fashioned. She wants that giant diamond on her finger."

"Her Hollywood boyfriend could have given her that."

"I wouldn't just take her word for it that *she* dumped *him*. She never struck me as the most truthful person. She reminds me of one of those femme fatale movie characters."

"May, stop worrying."

"She's trying to sink her hooks into you."

"You don't know that. And even if she were, I can take care of myself."

His sister shook her head. "Men have blind spots when it comes to women. You could have the IQ of Albert Einstein, but when you think with your dick, you're dumber than shit."

Kimani had been a blind spot, Ben thought to himself.

"I'm not interested in getting back together with Eumie," he tried to assure May.

"That's what you say now."

He gave her a chiding look, as if she were a petulant child unhappy with being told she had to do her homework before turning on the television. "She knows what I expect and don't expect. She's a grown woman. If she wants to risk getting hurt—"

"Wait, does that mean you're open to sleeping with her again?"

If May wasn't his sister and hadn't covered for him all those years when he'd snuck back into the house late after a night hanging with gang members, he would be tempted to take a paddle to her backside.

"She's coming with me to California, so—"

"What?! Why would you invite her to go with you, and when did you decide you're going back to California?"

"Our younger sister's homecoming is in a week. No one in our family is planning on visiting her except me."

During his four years at Howard, May and Uncle Gordon had been the only family members who had come to visit him. Ben had spent all the holidays with Uncle Gordon in California. Ben's father had not been pleased with his decision to turn down Oxford or an Ivy League school in favor of Howard.

"That doesn't explain why Eumie has to go."

"She's related to Aunt Alice," Ben said, referring to Uncle Gordon's wife, "and hasn't seen her in years."

"Related? She's something like a second cousin twice removed from Aunt Alice's cousin."

"Leave it, May. Like I said, I can handle myself."

May was quiet. Unlike their older sister, May knew when not to push things further with Ben. She would go boldly right up the edge of his patience, but she never crossed the line. She did, however, have the last salvo this time.

"So if Eumie is visiting Aunt Alice, that means you'll be in the San Francisco area," she said. "That's why you're brining Eumie."

Done with talking, he had closed his eyes, but he decided to humor her one last time. "What do you mean by that?"

"It's not like you can't get pussy wherever or whenever you want. So why Eumie? All I can think is that, somehow, she's a better safeguard for you when it comes to *her*."

Ben didn't say anything. He hadn't invited Eumie for that reason—at least not consciously.

May settled back into her chair. "Maybe I'll tag along, too. It might be fun to see what Eumie thinks of your San Francisco fucktoy."

Chapter Seven

After spending two days at UCLA with his youngest sister, Ben flew to San Francisco. Eumie behaved herself for the most part, even agreeing to watch a basketball practice. She spent most of the time on her mobile, but he appreciated that she didn't complain about boredom or ask to leave early. Her only comment about basketball was that it was too bad the players didn't get to have cute outfits like golfers did. Golf was the one sport Eumie was open to playing on occasion.

He had originally planned to be more involved in the Oakland waterfront property his family was developing, but after the article spotlighting his relationship to Uncle Gordon, he decided to take a lower profile. Nevertheless, he checked on the managers leading the project and agreed to a meeting with the San Francisco District Attorney's office.

In the Hall of Justice, he bumped into Claire, the barely legal blond whom Jake had acquired through the Scarlet Auction. She looked well and still sported the diamond and emerald ring she had worn her last day at Jake's cabin.

"Oh, hi," she greeted with a perky smile. "How've you been? Jake thought you and Jason had returned to China for good."

"Jason's in Singapore at the moment," Ben said.

Far away from Jake's influence, he added silently. After how things had ended at the cabin, his cousin had agreed to drop his friendship with Jake.

"You see a lot of Jake?" Ben asked.

"Yeah, we're, like, dating."

"Does the district attorney know that?"

"They asked if I was continuing my relationship with Jake, and I told them I was. It seems like they want to make the Scarlet Auction and the men involved out to be, like, bad, but it's all just a misunderstanding. I mean, I get that Montana—I forget her real name—and Jake didn't get along, but she signed up for the BDSM part, right?"

"So you didn't feel frightened during your time with Jake? You weren't worried that he would harm you?"

"That's exactly what the Assistant D.A. asked me. They played this audio recording of us—did you know we were being recorded?"

Ben stiffened. He hadn't known at the time, but one of the secret recording pens had been in his possession.

"Anyway," Claire continued, "they didn't tell me how or who did the recording, and I was gagging and crying on it, which was, like, kinda embarrassing to have that played in front of these lawyers, and I had to explain what BDSM was all about, like they weren't familiar with it, but it turns out they wanted to understand what my interpretation of it was. I mean, yeah, Jake was a tougher Dom than I thought. I thought he would be a little more gentle, like in the books, but it's kind of cool that he's, like, this super alpha kind of Dom."

Ben looked Claire over once more. As cute as she was, he didn't think she was the kind of woman to sustain Jake's interest for long. Jake was more likely keeping her on his good side during the D.A.'s investigation. Intentional or not, Claire had probably played a pivotal role in the plea deal Jake had gotten from the Trinity County D.A. She seemed smitten with Jake.

Ben's US attorney, Murray Jones, who had with him another attorney because he didn't specialize in criminal law, walked up at that point, and they headed into the meeting together. Claire waved a cheerful goodbye.

The meeting was not particularly enjoyable. The Assistant D.A., Tracy Clarkson, had chosen to treat Ben as a hostile witness, her judgment of Ben not unlike what Kimani's had first been.

"Were you a participant of the arrangement known as the Scarlet Auction?" asked Clarkson, a woman in her late thirties with the strong square jaw of certain European ancestry.

"I have never attended an auction of theirs," Ben replied.

"But you are aware of their activities?"

"I am aware they're no longer in operation."

"That does not mean we cannot hold the

organizers and any participants accountable for placing women in danger. Were you aware of their activities?"

Ben glanced at his attorney before answering, "I was."

"And do you condone their activities, Mr. Lee?"

"How are Mr. Lee's opinions pertinent to your investigation?" questioned the criminal attorney Jones had brought in.

"I'm under the impression that all the participants were willing and consented to their involvement," Ben said.

"So you think it's okay that women sell themselves to the highest bidder?"

"Do you believe the government should keep its laws off a woman's body?"

"Do you?"

"My client is here to cooperate with your investigation," interjected the criminal attorney, "not answer questions about his politics."

"Speaking of politics, I understand your uncle is running for mayor of Oakland."

Ben stiffened. "My uncle has nothing to do with any of this."

"Surely you are not threatening to smear an innocent man?" Jones asked.

"Of course not," she snapped, "but it might be unfortunate if our case moves forward and the nephew's involvement is mentioned in the press."

"I'd like a word with my client."

Ms. Clarkson motioned for her assistant to leave the room with her.

"I don't care if she wants to pin me with a prostitution charge," Ben said when he was alone with his attorneys, "but *none* of this hits Uncle Gordon."

"Technically, you exchanged no money with Miss Taylor," Jones said. "You and she were simply engaged in consensual sex."

"I don't think she'll be able to build a case and be ready to go public with it before the election," the second attorney said, "but if you're worried, you do have something of value to Ms. Clarkson that you could offer—the legal documents Miss Taylor signed."

Thanks to a hacker Stephens had employed, Ben had a copy of both the nondisclosure agreement and the questionnaire Kimani had filled out. On the latter, she had indicated a strong interest in almost all elements of BDSM. It was one of her many lies.

Ben rubbed his temples with his middle finger and thumb. He had committed his fair share of mistakes and done a great many stupid things, but Kimani Taylor was easily the biggest mistake he had ever made.

*****

"No ruling from the FPPC?" Ben asked his uncle after Aunt Alice and Eumie had left Gordon's office to get boba and milk tea down the street. Ben gazed out the window onto the floor of the headquarters, busy with volunteers that morning as they kicked off the weekend's precinct walking activities.

"Not yet," Uncle Gordon replied as he readied himself to pound the pavement for votes. "I bumped into a walker for Oakland Forward the other day."

After Ben had refused to take calls from Ezra Rosenstein, the committee chair for Oakland Forward had finally gotten the message that he shouldn't share any information about the PAC with Ben.

Ben's own pollster, who lived in Oakland, had mentioned that he had received two mailers from Oakland Forward. If the PAC was also hiring precinct walkers, that meant the committee had raised a decent sum of money so far.

Suddenly, Ben stiffened. His whole body turned hollow and hot at the same time. "What is *she* doing here?"

Uncle Gordon tried to follow Ben's line of sight. At first, he couldn't seem to find who Ben was referring to, but then he must have seen the woman in the red Stanford baseball cap with a curly ponytail sticking through the back.

"Ah, Montana," Uncle Gordon said. "I mean, Kimani."

Ben turned sharply to his uncle. "How do you know her name?"

"She told me."

Ben was stunned. "She told you?"

"She came to see me the other week."

Ben felt the hairs of his neck stand on end. What was she up to now? She would have heard about the impending closure of her paper. Was she trying to unearth more dirt in the hopes of keeping the paper alive?

"Turns out she's a reporter for the *Tribune*," Ben cautioned. "If I had known—"

"She told me," Uncle Gordon acknowledged in a tone devoid of anger or suspicion.

"She told you?" Ben repeated. "Why?"

"She came to apologize. Said the article that led to the FPPC investigation was her fault."

Ben was quiet. He hadn't expected that.

"I told her it doesn't matter whose fault it is." Gordon put a hand on Ben's shoulder. "I mean it. Finding fault compels one to stay in the past instead of moving forward."

"Analyzing the cause helps us to learn from our mistakes so we don't repeat them. I shouldn't have allowed her to get so close. I don't know why I trusted her."

"She said you didn't know she was a reporter and that you did nothing wrong—which is what I've always believed anyway—and she wanted to take the blame for that article."

"I knew something wasn't right about her, but I didn't act on my suspicions."

"I appreciate that you both want to claim credit for what happened, but it really doesn't help me."

"Did she say anything else?"

"She asked how you were doing."

His pulse quickened. Had she inquired after him to be polite or had she been truly interested in the answer?

"So you forgave her," Ben said. "What is she doing here now?"

They watched her receive a pile of door hangers from the precinct captain.

"It looks like precinct walking," Gordon replied, "though my staff is supposed to let me know about any new volunteers so that I can meet them personally to thank them. Or maybe it's part of the story she's working on."

Ben turned to his uncle again. "What?!"

"The *Tribune* is doing a profile of all the mayoral candidates."

"And you trust her and the *Tribune* to do this?"

"I read the *Tribune* quite often. They're an honest paper. And I don't see any reason not to trust Kimani."

Ben could hardly believe what his uncle was saying. He knew Uncle Gordon preferred to give people the benefit of the doubt, but he wasn't naïve. He came across mild-mannered, but that didn't mean he allowed people to take advantage of him. When going to bat for his clients, he was as much a bulldog as any hard-nosed, trash-talking, bloviating attorney— only more effective.

"I trust your judgment of people," Uncle Gordon added, "and you seemed to like her."

"That was before I knew what she was capable of."

Ben pressed his lips into a line and considered shutting the paper down without the two-week notice. He and Uncle Gordon watched her exchange smiles with the precinct captain, a good-looking African-

American male, before she pointed to another folder on the table behind the young man. It seemed like she said, "I'll take that one, too."

What the hell was she up to? And was she being friendly or was she flirting with the guy? Ben didn't like the way the young man's smile made him look more charming.

"Are you going to go over and say hello?" Uncle Gordon asked.

Ben drew in a sharp breath as he felt a throb in his chest. Though he had considered the many ways his paths might cross with hers, he had not concluded what he would actually do if they did meet. Uncle Gordon's campaign headquarters was one of the last places he would have expected to see Kimani.

Fuck.

His mind told him he should just skip what was sure to be an awkward and unpleasant moment, but every nerve of his was drawn to her. If he didn't take this chance, he'd be thinking about her every bloody minute for the rest of the day. Maybe he could tell if she was up to something questionable by her reaction to him.

He could imagine the look on her face when she realized she was caught with her hand in the cookie jar. She might think she could pull one over on his uncle, but she wasn't going to fool him a second time.

Straightening, he opened the office door and walked out onto the floor.

Chapter Eight

"**A**re you sure you want to do all those precincts?" the cute college grad asked with a smile that would make anyone who saw it brighten.

"I set aside the day to do this," Kimani replied.

"That's amazing of you, but we don't expect volunteers to do more than a precinct this morning, two at most."

"I'm a fan of Gordon Lee."

She didn't add that she also felt like she had to make it up to Gordon still.

"Well, you gotta be back for lunch," said Anthony. "We've got soul food for everyone walking today."

"I thought pizza was the staple of campaigns?"

"Yeah, but Maybelle is a big supporter of Gordon, and I'll take her barbecue over pizza any day."

Recalling the time she'd had lunch with Gordon and Ben, Kimani grew wistful. "I'd take her sweet potato pie over *anything* any day."

Anthony's smile grew even bigger. "You're my kind of woman."

Kimani returned an amused look. Was he flirting with her? She liked his affability, the sparkle of his eyes and that beautiful smile, but she had never considered dating a younger guy. Even though he was probably only about three years younger, she felt much older.

"You left your share of pie at my place."

She felt frozen to the spot while the coordination of her arms disappeared. Doorhangers and precinct folders slid to the floor.

Still rooted to the spot, she allowed Anthony to pick them up for her as her heart began to pound.

She couldn't believe it. It was him. Here. She thought he was in Hong Kong or Beijing. Why was he back already?

She turned around—and seeing Ben was like slamming into a brick wall. She couldn't even muster a fake smile and simple "hi."

His stare bore into her. It wasn't the same hungry-wolf look that she had been accustomed to seeing during her week with him, but it wasn't dissimilar, and it had the same effect of rattling her to the bones.

Anthony, having picked up on the words "my place," raised his brows. Ben didn't even look like he noticed Anthony, but Kimani knew Ben noticed a lot of things that other guys tended not to.

Somehow she had convinced herself that she was never going to see Ben again, so she had never prepared for what she would say if their paths did cross. From his lack of response to her messages and letter, she had assumed he wouldn't ever want to talk to her again.

Luckily, she was saved from the prolonged agony when a female campaign volunteer called out, "Anyone need a lift to their precinct?"

"I should grab her offer," Kimani said, turning to Anthony for the doorhangers and folders. She felt stupid for not even saying hello to Ben, but she didn't want to stick around.

"I'll help carry the stuff," Anthony offered.

"I've got it," Ben said sternly, perhaps the only person impervious to Anthony's smile.

Anthony handed over the stuff with a touch of reluctance. He held out his hand. "I'm Anthony, one of the precinct captains."

Ben looked at Anthony for the first time. He shook the young man's hand. "Ben. Lee."

"Oh! Are you related to Gordon?"

"He's my uncle."

Anthony brightened and shook hands more warmly. "Nice to meet you."

"I should catch my ride before she leaves," Kimani said. She tried to take the doorhangers and folders from Ben. "I can get these."

But he didn't release his hold of the materials. "I'll give you a lift."

No, no, no, no! She didn't want that. Several weeks ago, she had longed for the chance to talk to him, to tell him how sorry she was—face to face, not via a letter. But now that she had reconciled herself to the fact that she would never have that opportunity, now that she had accepted he probably hated her guts, she preferred that he was out of her life.

"I'm perfectly fine taking the bus, too," she said, "which is what I had planned on doing."

Ben ignored her. "Bataar has the car parked in front."

Her mouth went dry. *Hurry, think of something!*

As if sensing an alternative might prove helpful, Anthony said, "Or I can drive. In fact, given where you're walking, it's probably best you have someone with you."

That wasn't the solution she was looking for.

"I'm sure, as a precinct captain, you're needed here," Ben said to Anthony.

When she didn't budge, contemplating whether or not it was a good idea to take Anthony up on his offer, Ben grasped her elbow and guided her toward the doors. She opened her mouth to object at being dragged out as if she were a child refusing to leave the candy store. She wasn't his to boss around. She wasn't his...pet. Not anymore.

"I don't need a ride," she said when they were outside. She spotted his silver Porsche Panamera.

Whatever you do, girl, don't get in that car.

But maybe he just wanted to escort her off the premises because he didn't want her around him or his uncle. She couldn't blame him.

At the car, they stopped. She turned around. Meeting his gaze, she faltered. She couldn't make out the emotion in his eyes. Her insides crumbled, but mustering her courage, she said softly, "I tried to reach you, but I take it you didn't want to be reached—which I totally get."

Her words seemed to upset him, for he looked

away. A muscle tightened in his jaw. He turned back to her with a look that could have sliced steel.

Somehow, she pressed on, "But I was—"

"What are you doing here?" he interrupted.

She glanced at the doorhangers he held. "Trying to make things up to Gordon."

"You don't need to make anything up. In fact, it would be better if you didn't try to do anything at all where Uncle Gordon is concerned."

She drew in a painful breath. She deserved that. "A little precinct walking won't hurt."

His eyes narrowed. "I'm not sure I can believe you."

That hurt even more, but again, she deserved it. Her heart twisted in misery. Words couldn't express how bad she felt, but even if they could, she doubted she could find them. Her pulse was going at the speed of a NASCAR race because she realized he had drawn within inches of her, like he intended to pin her to the car. She remembered being caught between him and a car once.

Suddenly, she found it hard to breath, his presence drowning her. Part of her *wanted* his body to press her into the car. She wanted to drown. In him.

No, you don't.

Alarm bells went off in her head. He was trying to intimidate her, standing so close. She had tolerated his domination when she was playing the part of his submissive, but they weren't roleplaying anymore.

"It doesn't matter if you believe me or not," she

replied, sounding harsher than she'd intended because of her panic. She could feel his heat and energy in every molecule of air between them.

"I don't expect that you'll forgive me," she continued, "but I'm going to pass out these doorhangers. It's the least I can do."

His gaze seemed to search the depths of her eyes.

"And these precincts aren't getting done," she added.

He straightened to open one of the folders, providing an inch or two of space, enough for her to take a decent breath. He glanced at the map inside the folder with a neighborhood in East Oakland highlighted. Havenscourt.

"You're not walking here," he pronounced.

Now she was starting to get irritated. Why wouldn't he just leave her be?

"Why not?"

"Get a different precinct from that college kid."

Did that mean Ben was going to let her volunteer?

"East Oakland is not as bad as people think," she said. "And it's a Saturday morning."

He snapped the folder shut. "There are other precincts that haven't been walked."

"I don't think your uncle would want East Oakland ignored."

"The other precincts have more voters."

She lifted her chin. "All the more reason to walk East Oakland. There are plenty of potential voters there, but a lot of them feel disenfranchised, left out.

They don't feel empowered enough to believe their vote will make a difference."

"Elections are a numbers game. With limited time and limited resources, you want to aim for the highest, fastest returns. You can do voter registration outside of election season."

Although she usually enjoyed policy discussions, she didn't want to have one with Ben. She would have thought that Ben, having gone to Howard, would understand where she was coming from. But maybe she didn't know him as well as she thought. Being a billionaire from China still put him worlds apart from where she had grown up.

She reached for the doorhangers and folders. "I'm walking East Oakland."

How she thought she could wrestle the materials from him, she wasn't sure, but she wanted to find a way to end their conversation. She wanted to be on her way.

But he grabbed her wrist before she touched the doorhangers. Suddenly, only half an inch separated his body from hers. Adrenalin spiked through her, but, momentarily mesmerized by the emotion flaring in his eyes, she didn't try to escape.

"Benji!"

His hold on her wrist loosened, and she took the opportunity to both slip away and grab most of the doorhangers from him. A few fell to the ground, and she hurried to pick them up before they got dirty.

Having collected all the doorhangers, she stood

up to see a tall, beautiful woman approach Ben and wrap an arm around his waist. A few steps behind her was another Asian woman Gordon had introduced to the volunteers earlier as his wife, Alice Lee.

At the risk of appearing rude but realizing this was her chance to get away, Kimani said quickly, "I should get going to my precinct."

Campaign materials in hand, she scurried away.

"Who was that?" she heard the woman who could have been a Victoria Secret model say.

Kimani didn't hear Ben's reply, but her ears burned as she imagined the possible answers: damn reporter who can't be trusted, a pet I played with for a few days...nobody important.

The last one was probably the hardest to take.

*****

It had been dark for half an hour when Kimani decided to call it quits. She had passed out hundreds of doorhangers and spoken with dozens of registered voters. She had half the neighborhood to go, and then she would be completely done with the last precinct, but she couldn't shake the feeling that she was being watched again. Was she just being paranoid because of the break-in or was someone truly tailing her—and why? Had Jake hired someone just to spook her?

Marissa called her as she was taking the BART train back into San Francisco.

"When are you going to be back?" Marissa asked.

"I'm kind of nervous being home alone."

"I'm about thirty minutes away," Kim answered.

"God, I wish I hadn't given up smoking."

After hanging up, Kim leaned her head back against her seat. She felt bad for Marissa. None of this would be happening if she hadn't tried to expose the Scarlet Auction. Claire might have been just fine with Jake. Gordon would not be investigated by the FPPC, and though her efforts had landed her a job at the *Tribune*, she was going to end up unemployed soon anyway. Plus, she would never have met Ben.

If she could do it all over again...

But he gave you the most mind-blowing orgasms. You sure you would give those up?

Closing her eyes, she replayed her first time squirting. She had actually thought she had peed her pants, or *his* pants, rather. Jake had disallowed clothing for his subs, but Ben had lent her his sweats and shirt. Looking back, she should have seen earlier that he was different from Jake and the other two frat boys, Derek and Jason. But she had been prejudiced towards Ben, judging him guilty of assholeness by association and because he had offered to buy her for sex. The $200,000 he had paid for her could have gone toward a worthier cause.

So could the four dollars you spent on your morning latte. Who cares how much he spent? The guy made you squirt. And not just once.

A shiver went through her as she recalled her first night in his Pacific Heights penthouse. He had made her come ten times in succession that night. She would never have thought she could get exhausted through coming. She seemed to have an endless reservoir of arousal where he was concerned. He always found the right spots on, and in, her body, and he worked them relentlessly. She liked the way he dominated her—no, she loved the way he dominated her. She now fully understood why Marissa was so attracted to BDSM. Which shouldn't have surprised her that much because anything involving power was sexy, in money, politics, and sex itself.

Kim wondered if vanilla sex would prove too plain for her now. Would she need to search for future partners at places like The Lair? Would she find someone who could take her to the heights Ben had? Would she ever squirt again?

Feeling her carnal cravings begin to stir, she turned her mind to Gordon's campaign. What else could she do for him? She could walk all of Havenscourt herself, but she could tell that a number of the people she had spoken to were disinterested and a lot of the doorhangers she had passed out would probably end up in the trash.

"I don't vote anymore," one voter had said. "It hasn't changed a damn thing for me or the neighborhood. Just look at that basketball court there. It hasn't been fixed up in years. I'm not even sure it's safe for the kids to play on it."

"You want me to vote for a Chinese guy? What's he going to do for our community?" asked another.

"I'm a Republican, so my vote doesn't matter since a Republican hasn't won in Oakland since...probably since before I was born!"

"I understand where you're coming from," Kimani had said to the first apathetic voter. "This community has so many needs that haven't been addressed. But if you don't vote, for sure things will just stay the same."

She thought about the basketball court in the center of the neighborhood and how it was just one of many things that could benefit from attention, but she understood that government resources, even in a city where voters were not adverse to raising taxes, were far short of what was needed.

Kimani sat up. Maybe she could organize an event to draw attention to the dilapidated basketball court. And if she could involve Gordon's campaign, he'd get visibility, too—a win-win.

The more she dwelled on her idea, the more excited she became. The campaign could register voters at the event. Maybe it could even raise funds to at least fix the holes in the fence and put actual nets on the hoop.

She couldn't wait to pitch her idea to Gordon. He might say that he doesn't have the time or staff to dedicate to such an event, but she would offer to organize it. She could get her parents, Keisha, and other folks she knew to help out.

The biggest potential challenge she faced was getting past Ben.

Chapter Nine

Pissed that Kimani had gotten away from him, and that she had defied his directive not to walk East Oakland, Ben took his frustrations out on the precinct captain back inside the headquarters.

"You let a young woman walk Havenscourt alone?" he barked at Anthony, wanting to fire the guy for having such a winning smile.

"I offered to go with her," Anthony replied. "Should I go get her?"

Imagining the young man getting chummy with Kimani, Ben replied, "No. But don't let her do it again."

Anthony nodded. "Got it."

Ben turned around and blew out a breath. Bill was supposed to be on Kimani, so she wasn't really alone. Still...

"Who was she?" Eumie tried again, trying not to appear too curious.

"A campaign volunteer," Ben replied as he texted Bataar to confirm that Bill was watching Kimani.

Eumie swirled the ice in her drink. "It looked like she was more than just a volunteer. It looked like you had some history with her."

After receiving confirmation from Bataar, Ben looked up from his mobile at Eumie. "You could say that."

"That's it? You're just going to leave it at that?"

"Yes, I am."

She pouted but didn't back down. "Was your history a dating history?"

He couldn't help a rueful laugh. "Hardly."

Her brow furrowed in puzzlement. "Then what was it?"

"I'm not interested in talking about it."

While he would have tolerated some pushback from May, he would put Eumie back on a plane to China within minutes if she persisted.

Getting the message, she muttered, "Must have been some history."

Ben regretted allowing Eumie to accompany him to California. At least May hadn't pushed to come along. She wouldn't have lasted five minutes with Eumie.

"I didn't know you were interested in her kind. Was it because you went to Harvard?" Eumie asked.

"Howard. It was Howard University." He looked at the time on his mobile. "I'm meeting a property owner in Chinatown for dim sum. I can have Bataar drop you off at Union Square."

Eumie's activity of choice in any metropolitan area was shopping. She rarely did the tourist attractions, had no interest in museums, and refused to walk anywhere she couldn't wear her four-inch heels.

"Thanks," she said. "Aunt Alice offered to give me a ride, but I think she drives a Honda Accord. The

Porsche is a much better ride."

Ben turned to head outside.

Eumie finished her sugary beverage of milk tea and boba. "Should we meet for dinner? You think you could get a table at Ishikawa West?"

He froze, remembering how hot Kimani had looked the night he'd taken her to the Michelin-star restaurant. He remembered making her sit on his lap while the servers cleared the table because she had complained about appearing like a couple having an argument. He remembered the punishment afterward when—

"You have to book six weeks in advance," he abruptly said to Eumie before his mind went too far down memory lane.

"Yes, but I know you can pull strings." She ran a finger down his arm. "Come on."

"I don't feel like Japanese. We can pick up noodles and have dinner back at my place."

Eumie wrinkled her nose. "I can get noodles back home."

"And you had plenty of sushi and kaiseki in Tokyo."

She sighed. "Fine, but let's at least order something fancier than noodles."

Her statement reminded him of how impressed Kimani had been by the hole-in-the-wall noodle house he had taken her to their first night in San Francisco.

After Eumie was seated in the Porsche, Bataar closed her door and pulled Ben aside. "Given what Jake might be up to, I should be covering *you*, not chauffeuring Miss Ma."

"Jake doesn't have the guts or wherewithal to do anything to me. And you're just dropping her off. Wong can pick her up," Ben replied. Wong was his driver.

Bataar continued to frown.

"This isn't Hong Kong," Ben said, "and my meeting is in Oakland Chinatown. Nothing's going to happen."

"All right, boss, as long as I don't have to stay with Miss Ma—not that I wouldn't mind watching her ass all day—"

Ben snorted. "I'm sure you wouldn't."

"But you're my priority."

"Kimani's your priority," Ben reminded him. "I want to know she made it back safely."

Bataar nodded before getting into the car behind the wheel. Eumie waved at Ben from the passenger side.

After they drove away, Ben contemplated going into Havenscourt himself. She shouldn't be anywhere near Uncle Gordon or his campaign...but he believed her. He could see the contrition in her eyes.

But he had trusted her before. And got burned for it. With Uncle Gordon paying the price.

To be safe, he should pull her out of East Oakland and slap a restraining order on her. He recalled Uncle Gordon saying something about a profile the *Tribune* was doing. What the hell was that all about?

He wanted to ask her about that, but did he really want to come within ten feet of her again? Like a shark scenting blood, his arousal had perked the instant he'd caught a whiff of her. No perfume, just the faint fragrance of her soap or body wash. And all her.

When he had caught her wrist, he had managed to yank her just short of him. But what he'd really wanted was to feel her body crashing into his. He wanted to slam her against the car, maul her, grope her, kiss her till she cried.

Fuck.

How was it his reaction to her seemed even stronger now than before?

Tension coiled inside his body, and sex with Eumie wasn't going to be enough to relieve him. He hoped Bataar was up for a beating, or maybe Bataar would be open to beating the shit out of *him*. Then maybe, just maybe, he might find relief.

*****

"What happened to you?" Eumie asked when she entered Ben's place in Pacific Heights to find him sitting on the sofa with an icepack to the side of his head.

"Nothing," Ben replied. "Bataar and I had a vigorous sparring match."

When they sparred, both men held back as it wasn't necessary or advisable to go all out. But this time, Ben had wanted Bataar to go hard. He'd had to bait Bataar to do it.

"Don't you hate watching me fuck all these women without being able to join in on the fun?" Ben had asked when deriding the Mongolian's kicks as "weak-assed" and his right hooks as "pussy punches" hadn't worked.

Bataar had grinned. "Think of me as a parent living vicariously through his son's sports accomplishments."

"You're not resentful that you don't even get sloppy seconds?"

"That was never listed as a job perk," Bataar had returned after dodging a roundhouse kick.

Referring to Bataar's mother hadn't worked, either. No matter how aggressive Ben had gotten with his strikes and kicks, Bataar had refused to engage his full strength. He would allow himself to get beaten black and blue before taking out his boss.

However, Ben had managed to find a weak spot.

"That niece of yours is almost eighteen now, right?" Ben had said. "You think she might ever be open to BDSM? I'd—"

And that was all it had taken for Bataar to knock Ben on his arse. He knew Ben never played with jailbait or anyone close to that age, but he had obviously wanted to get the right message across just in case.

"You know I don't mess with women that young," Ben had affirmed to Bataar as they sat on the gym mats afterward, both of them bruised and sweating. "They're still too innocent."

"Even if my niece were sixty years old, I wouldn't want you touching her," Bataar had answered between hard breaths.

Ben remembered warning Kimani that he wouldn't trust his own sisters to someone like himself. But Kimani had stayed anyway, even though she had been given the chance to walk away. At the time, his emotions had swelled, thinking that she had chosen to be with him despite whatever reservations she'd had. Turned out she had simply chosen to continue her charade so she could get her scoop for the *Tribune*.

But she couldn't fake her orgasms that well. She couldn't fake squirting. So while her job and the paper might have been her prime motivators, she wasn't immune to him. He had sensed it still today outside the campaign headquarters. The current between them flowed both ways.

"I'm starving," Eumie pronounced, setting down her shopping bags from Neiman Marcus and Burberry. "Did you pick up food?"

"I'm taking you out for dinner," he replied. Initially, he had opted for takeout so that he and Eumie could get to the sex sooner rather than later. Dinners with Eumie weren't that interesting. They would each end up spending most of the time on their respective mobile devices.

At the moment, however, he wasn't that interested in sex with Eumie.

Eumie brightened. "Oh, good. Where?"

"Come up with your top favorites, and Beth will try to get a reservation at one of them."

He picked up his land line and dialed his personal assistant, giving her instructions before handing the phone to Eumie.

"There's so many to choose from," Eumie said. "Do I feel like fusion or French or Californian? We are in California, after all."

While Eumie prattled aloud, Ben texted Bataar:

> Where's my update on
> Kimani?

Half a minute later, he received his answer:

> She just arrived home.

Ben glanced at the time on his mobile, got up and decided to call Bataar from his room.

"She's getting home late," Ben said to Bataar, tossing aside his ice pack.

"Teenagers stay out later than this, boss."

"Where was she?"

"Doing her precinct walking."

Ben felt his entire body tense. "Are you fucking with me? She was out walking Havenscourt at this hour?"

That Anthony kid was about to lose his job as a precinct captain.

"I switched out Bill for Moe, given where she was

spending her time. She's fine. There were no incidents. Bill's going to watch her the rest of the night."

"Didn't she return to the campaign headquarters for lunch?"

"She stopped at a hot dog stand for her lunch and kept on going."

A part of Ben was disappointed that he didn't have an excuse to fire Anthony, even though he really wasn't in a position to fire staff that wasn't his. But he doubted his uncle would stop him.

"She walked Havenscourt the whole day?" Ben asked.

"If anything suspicious happens, I'll let you know."

"I want a daily report."

"I'll confirm when she's safely tucked in bed every night."

Ben didn't feel satisfied, however. He didn't want her walking Havenscourt or any part of East Oakland again, but he wasn't her fucking dad.

Eumie walked in at that moment. "Beth got us a reservation, but it's not for another hour, so we have time..."

She wrapped her arms around his waist.

"I have some things to take care of before dinner," he told her.

She appeared startled. He doubted few men ever passed on an opportunity to bed her.

"Like what?" she asked.

"You really want to go into it?"

She pressed herself closer to him. "Oh, you mean

boring stuff. And you're choosing to do that over..."

"'Boring stuff' still needs to get done."

She tilted her head to one side as she studied him. "You're not like the Ben I knew. The old Ben always found time to fit in a quickie, though I love that your quickies are longer than what most guys would call a full session."

Her hand drifted to his crotch. He caught her by the wrist.

"I'm not in the mood, Eumie."

"Men are always in the mood," she retorted.

He saw that she wasn't going to relent anytime soon. It was a matter of pride more than pleasure right now. It would be a large blow to her ego if she couldn't successfully seduce him.

"After dinner," he offered, wanting to check in with Stephens. Earlier, he had asked him to dig up what he could about the article the *Tribune* was doing on Uncle Gordon. Halting the paper would be easier, and the attorney who'd handled the acquisition had said there would be no problems in doing so.

"You want to pay a bunch of journalists to do nothing, that's your prerogative. Their guild can't complain you didn't give them proper notice since they're technically still on payroll," the attorney had said.

Uncle Gordon, who believed Kimani and the *Tribune* had only honorable intentions, might be disappointed, but it was better to err on the side of caution. They had already been burned. There was no reason to keep the paper going.

Except that Ben was sure Kimani enjoyed her job. She would probably work for free if she could.

"Can't your boring stuff wait?" Eumie persisted.

She had a point. It could wait. He didn't want to wait, but maybe he should just do Eumie right now so she would stop pestering him.

Still holding her by the wrist, he yanked her body around. She yelped as she collided into him. He tossed his mobile onto the bed. A brief smile of triumph brightened her expression before he caught her by the back of her neck with his other hand and crushed his mouth atop hers.

"You sure you want this?" he murmured over her lips. "You might regret it."

She returned a quizzical look, but he wasn't going to explain himself. She had a chance to back out. When she didn't say anything, he grabbed her arse through her skin-tight leggings and ground his burgeoning erection against her.

"Now this is the Ben I know," she purred.

He moved his hand to her jaw, cupping her tightly. Her eyes widened in alarm.

"We do this quickie my way."

"It's always your way, Benji," she murmured through his grip squishing her cheeks together.

Letting her go, he pulled her top over her head and just down past her shoulders, letting the form-fitting garment imprison her arms. He eyed the breasts protruding from her pink lace push-up bra. He palmed one of them, grazing his thumb over the nipple. With her new boob job, she didn't need to wear a push-up bra, but she probably figured more cleavage was always better than less. He pushed the bra up over her breasts, then squeezed both of the freed orbs. She closed her eyes and moaned as he fondled her.

Her eyes flew open when he pinched a nipple hard.

She needed to learn not to mess with him. He knew by ravishing her, he was proving her point that men could always be put in the mood for sex, but she was going to rethink her persistence next time.

He pinched the other nipple, making her cry out.

He pushed her down to her knees and pulled down his sweats. Eumie wasn't keen on giving blow jobs, but he presented his stiffened cock. When she stared at it reluctantly, he gave her a light slap on the cheek. She opened her mouth...and gagged the instant his cock grazed her tongue.

"I see your Hollywood boyfriend didn't train you well," he said.

She glared at him. "I have a sensitive throat. You know that. And he wasn't into this kind of stuff."

What kind of wuss wasn't into blow jobs? No matter.

"We can make up for that," he told her.

She wrinkled her nose, which he pinched shut to get her to open her mouth. He didn't push himself in the way he had that day at Jake's cabin, when the four women were all giving head to see who could get their man off first. Jason had come first, but Ryan had been deemed the winner because Lisa hadn't swallowed every last drop of Jason's cum.

Ben forgot how many times he had orgasmed in Kimani's mouth before he had finally ejaculated. It hadn't been easy for her to keep up with him, but she had been a trooper, sucking him hard in an effort to pull him over the edge. The visual of her supple lips wrapped about his shaft was almost enough to make him come, but he wasn't going to let Eumie off that easy.

Eumie continued to gag, and she hadn't yet mastered how to keep her teeth from scraping him, but he pressed himself farther into her mouth anyway. Cupping the back of her head, he guided her up and down his length, occasionally giving her a break to recover from her choking.

"Learned your lesson yet?" he asked.

Saliva and pre-cum glistened on her lower lip. She nodded.

"Let's be extra sure," he said, shoving his cock back into her mouth.

By the time he decided she'd had enough, tears had formed in the corners of her eyes. He dragged her over to the bed, sat down, and hauled her face down over his lap. He yanked her leggings down past her rump.

"What—what are you doing now?" she asked in a panic.

"Continuing your lesson," he answered, then gave

a buttock a sound smack.

She yelped. "Don't you bruise me!"

"Unless you're modeling naked, a bruise on your arse isn't going to hurt."

Well, it might hurt receiving one.

"Ai-yah!" she cried out when he spanked her.

Unlike their sex in Tokyo last week, he managed to keep his frustrations under control this time. Sparring with Bataar had released some of his inner turmoil, though hearing that Kimani had been walking Havenscourt at night had set off a new round of stress.

Kimani should be the one splayed over his knees, Kimani receiving the spanking, Kimani whimpering beneath his hand, moaning at his touch, orgasming around his cock, coming undone in his arms.

He took a break from spanking Eumie to fit his hand between her arse cheeks and the waistband of her leggings and found that, despite her crying and wailing, she was wet. He teased more wetness from her by playing with her clit. She whimpered, this time from pleasure.

As he stood, he pulled her up and saw that her tears had fallen, bringing a little of her mascara down toward her cheeks. His cock fully hard now, he pushed her face down onto the bed and pulled her onto her knees by her hips. He could teach her a really hard lesson by taking her arse. Her pale white backside, now glowing pink and crimson, beckoned, but he would bet that Eumie was not a virgin there.

After getting on a condom, he sank his cock into

her pussy. She was nice and hot.

He was about to lean over and fondled her clit when a short bell went off on his mobile. It was a text from Bataar:

> Kimani and her roommate left the
> house.

Placing one hand on Eumie's lower back to hold her in place, he went slow and gentle till he had her purring. With his other hand, he picked up his mobile and texted back:

> Where are they headed?

He waited a long two minutes before Bataar replied:

> Bill heard them mention
> someplace called The Lair.

Chapter Ten

"Am I sure I want to do this?" Kimani asked herself in the mirror. She reviewed her outfit. What did one wear to a BDSM club? In her skinny jeans and cold-shoulder top, she looked like she could be headed to a ballgame. She wore her hair down with minimal styling and a headband to keep her curls from falling into her face. She looked over at Marissa, who wore leather leggings and a red strapless top.

"We don't have to do anything. In fact, these days I just go to watch. I haven't played since..." began Marissa, as she touched up her makeup. "I'm hoping I can play someday soon. If I can do that, I'll be back to the way I was."

Kimani bit her bottom lip. After what Marissa had been through, could one ever go back to being the way they were?

"I'm sorry," Kimani said. "I'm sure the break-in isn't helping things."

Marissa put her lipstick back in her purse. "Why are you sorry? It's not your fault our place got broken into."

Kimani drew in a deep breath. It wasn't right not telling Marissa. "It *is* my fault. It's because I did the Scarlet Auction."

Marissa tilted her head. "You did what?"

"After you told me what had happened to you, I started looking into the Scarlet Auction. It sounded really shady to me, so I went undercover to try to expose them. I didn't bring you up at all, and I wasn't going to mention you in the scoop. I was going to keep you out of everything."

"What do you mean? How were you going to expose the Scarlet Auction?"

"I pretended to be a participant. I got bid on and bought by a guy who turned out to be a total asshole. He's the one behind the break-in. The only thing taken was my laptop. The guy's probably worried I'm going to write a tell-all article about him."

Marissa sat down at the kitchen table as she tried to take in everything.

"I ended up pressing charges against him up in Trinity County."

"So that's how you really got your bruise?"

Kimani nodded, also taking a seat at the table.

"Your guy was just like mine? I wonder if he's the same guy?"

"Yours sounded older, but I'm not surprised I found a jerk. It was just like I expected or hoping for. Guess I gotta be careful what I wish for. I didn't get beat up as much as you did, thanks to another guy who intervened. If that guy hadn't been there... I try not to think about it. It rattles you to the core. At first, I started seeing every guy as if he were Jake, the guy who bought me. Even now, I wonder about men—the guy behind me in the grocery line, or the pedestrian yelling into his cellphone, I wonder if these men are like him deep down."

"What happened when you pressed charges?"

"He reached a plea deal with the district attorney for a fine and a restraining order."

"See, that's probably what would happen if I tried to press charges. It's not worth it."

"Well, if you change your mind—"

"Why would I want to do that? I'd have to give the Scarlet Auction back their money if they found out I broke the nondisclosure agreement. I can't afford it. I'd have to stop seeing my therapist. Besides, I'm trying to put it behind me, not relive the shit."

Kimani said nothing. When Marissa had first confessed what had truly happened to her, she had been appalled that her roommate wasn't pressing charges against her abuser, but she was now more sympathetic toward Marissa's position. Having gone through the process, it hadn't been fun, to say the least. And the result was hardly satisfying. Still, she wouldn't have done it any other way. The public needed to know what Jake was capable of, and hopefully soon, the Scarlet Auction would be held publicly accountable as well.

"So are you, like, doing a story on the Scarlet Auction?" Marissa asked.

"Not yet. I passed the info on to the San Francisco D.A., and she asked the paper to hold off on anything, so you can't tell anyone that the D.A. is investigating the Scarlet Auction."

"It's too bad. It was a neat concept. I guess we weren't one of the luckier women."

"I don't know if there are *any* lucky women in this whole setup."

Silence settled between them until Kimani said, "I did get something out of it though—a newfound appreciation for kink."

"You mean tonight wouldn't be your first night with BDSM?"

"The guy who saved me from Jake, he showed me a thing or two."

Marissa's mood lightened. "Really? Do tell."

"I think our ride is here."

They gathered their things and stepped outside to find their taxi waiting for them.

"But I'm going with you to The Lair to provide moral support," Kimani added before getting into the taxi.

"Well, maybe you'll decide to join in."

Kimani smiled. "That's a big maybe."

Chapter Eleven

Ben had stopped thrusting, the whirling of his mind taking precedent. He was fully familiar with The Lair. Why was Kimani headed there? Was she a member? He had gotten the impression she was a BDSM novice. Her answers saying she was into all sorts of kink on the Scarlet Auction questionnaire, from multiple partners to golden showers, had all been lies.

But maybe she was more interested in BDSM than he had thought. After all, she'd been receptive to everything he had done with and to her.

Jealousy simmered as he wondered if she had a partner at The Lair—not something he wanted to be thinking about.

"Benji?" Eumie murmured, her face still smushed into his comforter.

He texted Bataar back:

You sure?

Bataar responded:

I'll have Bill confirm when they arrive at their destination.

Setting down his mobile, he pulled out of Eumie to reach into his bedside drawer and pull out a cordless vibrator. Switching it on, he held it between her legs. She immediately began purring. Her moans doubled in volume when he sank himself back into her wet heat. While holding the vibrator between her pussy lips, he rolled his hips.

He thought about asking Bataar if Bill planned to go into The Lair with Kimani, then he could report back with what she did, who she was with.

But that would be stalking, and it would make him as much of a creep as Jake. And what did he care what she did and whom she did it with? He was responsible for keeping her safe from Jake. That was it. If she wanted to be foolhardy and walk Havenscourt at night, that shit was on her.

Eumie started screaming and convulsing. He held the wand in place till she couldn't stand the vibrations, then he lowered the setting and eventually withdrew the device. Pulling out of her, he jacked himself off. For a few minutes, nothing but pleasure rippled through him, washing away all thoughts of Kimani and The Lair.

Eumie had collapsed onto the bed, her arms still pinioned behind her by her top. Tossing the condom, Ben lay down on the bed. Maybe it hadn't been wise to come back to the Bay Area, but he couldn't have predicted that he would bump into Kimani. And at Uncle Gordon's campaign headquarters, of all places.

She had walked the entire day. In East Oakland.

There weren't that many volunteers who would do that. Maybe she was sincere in her desire to help Uncle Gordon.

He picked up his mobile and texted Bataar:

> Tell me about her walk.

Bataar returned:

> She hung doorhangers and talked to people.

Ben texted:

> Your guy Moe hear what she said?

Bataar replied:

> He got close once when he saw a pit bull come around a house. Luckily, the owner was able to call the dog back. She talked about how your uncle was the right person to be mayor.

Eumie snuggled up to him.

"I've got to make a call," he said, getting up.

"At least help me with my top," she said.

He pulled her garment down her arms and went into the bathroom.

"Our hacker got into the *Tribune's* server," Stephens said. "There's a document that looks like a draft of the article you're looking for. I'll send it to you."

She was working as a volunteer and writing an article on Uncle Gordon? That had to be a conflict of interest. But he felt less anxious about the need to shut down the paper. Maybe she'd been telling the truth in that letter she'd sent him. She really did feel bad about that article on Gordon and Oakland Forward.

He hadn't believed her. Or maybe he hadn't *wanted* to believe her. He hadn't forgiven himself for what had happened, so why should he forgive *her*?

"See if you can find out when the article is scheduled to run," he instructed Stephens.

Eumie entered then. She had stripped down to nothing and looked at herself in the mirror, her favorite activity of all time.

"Did you have to spank so hard?" she asked as she examined the reflection of her arse.

"Be happy I didn't spank you hard enough to bruise," he replied.

She pouted at him before turning on the shower. "You want to take one together?"

He instantly recalled the time he and Kimani had showered together. He had held her up by the legs to one of the jets. Her wet body quaking in his arms had been one of his favorite moments. So was the time he'd bound her to a chair on Jake's boat. She had been wearing a bikini borrowed from Jason's sub, Lisa, a waif compared to the other women. Kimani's baps were overflowing the top, and the boyshorts molded her arse like second skin. He had stuffed the bikini bottom into her mouth before pumping himself into her.

He had taught her how to water-ski that day. The glow of accomplishment when she had learned to get up on the water had been beautiful. Almost as good as fucking her.

Then there was the time they'd shot hoops together on his patio. The time he'd aroused her in the bathroom of a coffee shop. Their dinner at a hole-in-the-wall in Chinatown. The first time she'd begged for his cock. The sound of her calling him "Master."

Bloody good times.

"You go ahead," Ben told Eumie. "I need to review a document."

On his mobile, he pulled up the file Stephens had sent him. The article started with Gordon's past, how he put himself through college and law school while working two low-wage jobs; his work as an attorney representing tenants, which included Maybelle, with quotes of her praising Gordon; and other pro-bono jobs he had taken on. But the article also quoted his critics, including community advocates who felt he had approved too many pro-business projects during his time on the Planning Commission. The article also cited the ongoing FPPC investigation.

As far as reporting went, Ben had to admit it was a fair and unbiased article, and it showed a side of Gordon many may not have been aware of, the human side of a man who came across as a nerdy bureaucrat.

But voters didn't need to be reminded of the FPPC investigation. And this article was in draft form. Who knew what it would read like after it was finalized and edited?

Better to be safe than sorry.

Ben dialed the attorney. "Shut the paper down."

Chapter Twelve

To protect the confidentiality of its patrons, The Lair required all guests to put their phones, cameras and other valuables in cubbies near the entrance. Kimani didn't know what to expect, since Marissa had never described the place in detail, but the woman who greeted them was friendly and dressed as if she were a hostess at a restaurant.

"Are we in need of partners this evening?" asked the greeter, holding up different colored wristbands.

Marissa hesitated.

"This is my first time," Kimani replied, "so I guess I'm just checking things out."

The woman handed her a white wristband and a green one. "The green one is for first-timers. The white one signals that you're not playing tonight. If you change your mind, just come see me."

She turned to Marissa, who said, "I'll take a white one for now."

As Kimani put on her wristbands, she observed a woman wearing a trench coat and black leather boots.

"Good evening, ma'am," the greeter said to the woman with a regal carriage.

The woman looked over at Marissa and Kimani before settling her gaze on Marissa. The right corner of her lips curled slightly, and her eyes brightened with appreciation. But she said nothing as she went up a set of stairs behind the greeter.

Kimani turned to Marissa. "Where do the stairs lead to?"

"The Upper Balcony," Marissa replied as she led Kimani past the greeter and down the steps to the main area. "Upper Balcony is for the VIP members only. I'd like to go up there one day, but I'm not even sure how one gets to be a VIP member."

Kimani had half expected to walk into a room full of BDSM equipment not unlike what she'd seen in Ben's playroom, but the main floor resembled a hotel lobby with nicely appointed sitting areas and a sideboard with a water dispenser and bowls of gummy bears. Nondescript music with a throbbing beat played in the background.

"Why gummy bears?" Kimani asked as she helped herself to a cup of water at the sideboard.

"Sugar helps keep your energy level up," Marissa explained, "and you really don't want to eat anything too substantive, especially if you're doing a long anal session."

Kimani remembered the time Ben had sank himself there. It had been more amazing than she'd ever thought possible.

"Cold?" Marissa asked after noticing Kimani had shivered.

"I'm good," Kimani answered.

A woman wearing a black bustier and five-inch stilettos came up to the sideboard. She gave Kimani a broad smile before checking out the wristbands she wore.

"First time? Welcome," she said. "I hope you like what you see."

"Thanks," Kimani replied.

The woman swept her gaze over Kimani and flashed her another smile before wandering off.

"Oh my God, she was totally checking you out," Marissa giggled. "I thought she was going to hit on you, even though you're wearing a white wristband."

Kimani fingered the wristband. "So this is my shield?"

"Sort of."

"So where does all the, uh, action happen?"

Marissa pointed to the far wall of curtains. "Behind there."

"Do you want to go there now?"

Marissa hesitated again. "Let's just finish our water here first."

They sat down on a divan. Kimani looked at the oil paintings on the walls. One was of a naked woman dangling upside down from the ceiling high above a crowd of people in an 18th-century ballroom. Beside it was a painting of a naked man bent and tied to an A-frame. On the opposite wall, one painting depicted a woman being ravished by a satyr, while, in another, three nymphs bathed near a waterfall while three men looked on, their hands around their cocks.

Two men emerged from behind the curtains. One wore jeans and a cowboy hat. The other wore nothing at all except for a collar about his neck.

"Is that Marissa?" the naked one asked, coming up to them. "Girl, I haven't seen you in a while."

Marissa returned a small smile. "Busy, I guess."

The man furrowed his brow. "How can you be too busy for The Lair? That's a travesty. And is that a *white* wristband? I've never seen you wear a white one before."

"I'm showing a friend around," Marissa said before introducing Kimani to Matthew, who introduced his partner, Caleb. They shook hands as casually as if they were meeting at a coffee shop.

"Well, I hope your friend lets you get your usual red wristband before the night's over," Matthew said with a wink before he and Caleb went on their way.

"What do the red wristbands mean?" Kimani asked.

"It means you're hardcore and seeking a partner."

"What if you're not seeking a partner?"

"Either you have a white wristband or you have a collar. Collars mean you're taken."

They finished their water. Marissa got a few gummy bears before declaring that she was ready to proceed.

They stepped behind the curtains and were instantly greeted by the sight of three women in the center of the room. The Mistress from the sideboard sat on a Victorian sofa, her legs spread wide open to accommodate a brunette going to town on her. A young blond suckled her breasts.

Warmth crept up Kimani's cheeks. Though she had witnessed Ryan going down on Claire on Jake's boat, she still wasn't that used to seeing other people engaged in sex, up close and in person. Looking past the trio of women, she took in several alcoves surrounding more than half the room. The alcoves each had curtains, providing the occupants privacy if they so choose. The occupants in the right corner alcove had chosen to kept their curtains open. In it, a dominatrix flogged a tall and lanky male. Kimani noticed the woman used a flogger with wide falls, not unlike the one Ben had used on her. She had actually liked the feel of the flogger and wondered if she could enjoy the implement no matter who wielded it.

Seeing another sideboard with water and gummy bears, and needing something to do besides gawk, Kimani and Marissa went over and helped themselves to more water.

"Do you opt for new partners each time?" Kimani asked.

"Not always," Marissa replied. "I had a steady partner for a while, but he moved to—no, there he is!"

Kimani followed Marissa's gaze to a tan, dark-haired young man examining the different floggers at a counter. As if he felt their gazes, he turned around. It took him a few seconds in the dim lighting but then recognition seemed to dawn. Setting down the flogger he held, he walked over.

"Marissa," he greeted warmly.

"Miguel," she replied, returning a shy smile. "I

thought you were in San Diego?"

"I moved back. The startup wasn't working out, but I got a job offer here."

"Miguel, this is my roommate, Kimani. It's her first time, so I'm playing tour guide."

They shook hands.

"So you're not playing?" Miguel asked, eying Marissa's white wristband.

Marissa shook her head. "Not tonight."

Just then, a sexy young redhead dressed in a skintight cocktail dress appeared before them. "Ladies."

She presented a silver tray with an envelope on it. With a quizzical look, Marissa took the enveloped and opened it. Her mouth dropped open as she read the card inside.

"It's an invitation to the Upper Balcony!" she gasped.

Miguel looked surprised. "I didn't know one could get invited to the Upper Balcony."

"Neither did I."

"Someone must like you two."

Marissa turned to the redhead. "Who's it from?"

"I can't reveal the names of the members unless they wish to be known," replied the redhead.

"Why do they want to invite us?" Kimani asked, wanting to add, *And what are they expecting?*

"I haven't been told."

Marissa held the card to her chest. "I've always wanted to see what the Upper Balcony was like."

"Then what are you waiting for?" Miguel encouraged.

Marissa asked the redhead, "Do you think we could extend the invitation to include Miguel?"

"I'll have to check," replied the redhead.

"I so want to know who the invitation is from!" Marissa said while they waited for the redhead to return with an answer.

"Hopefully not a creep," Kimani replied, but then she remembered the woman at the entrance. *Women can be creeps, too*, she reminded herself.

"I think VIP members are heavily vetted and screened," Miguel said. "At least, that's what I've been told."

Kimani looked over at Marissa, "You can never be too sure these days."

"I don't expect to do anything in the Upper Balcony," Marissa said. "I just want to see what it's like."

"I don't know. We have no idea who this person is."

"I'm not so worried. There are bouncers everywhere in case anyone gets out of hand."

Marissa gestured to the far corner, and that's when Kimani noticed a muscled man in the shadows.

"Still, I've had enough surprises to last me a lifetime."

Marissa sighed. "Yeah, you're right. Maybe we should play it safe."

Miguel looked stunned. "Are you saying you're

going to pass up an invitation to the Upper Balcony? It's only the most exclusive BDSM spot in the city— maybe the whole state!"

Marissa bit her bottom lip. She looked at Kimani. "What should I do?"

The redhead returned with an answer. "The gentleman is invited as well on one condition."

Surprise, Kimani thought wryly to herself. She didn't want to be a wet blanket, but after what she and Marissa had been through, it was better to be safe than sorry.

The redhead looked at Kimani. "The member would like *you* to wait in the Silk Room. Alone."

Double surprise. Kimani had guessed the woman at the entrance was more interested in Marissa, but maybe she had thought wrong. Still, she balked, "No way I'm going to be locked alone in a room with a stranger."

"There are no doors and locks at The Lair," the redhead said. "Only curtains. And our security is always on hand. Our visitors forego some privacy, but we prioritize safety."

"Don't worry about me," Miguel said. "You should enjoy your invitation the way you want it."

Marissa frowned. "I don't know...maybe it's not such a big deal to go to the Upper Balcony."

"Not a big deal?" Miguel exclaimed. "Marissa, I'm excited you get to go. It'll be the highlight of my night to hear you tell me all about it."

"But I don't want Kimani to—"

"I'll go," Kimani blurted, not wanting to ruin what could be Marissa's only chance to see the Upper Balcony. "But I want a bouncer stationed right outside this Silk Room."

But what if the bouncer couldn't be trusted? What if this mysterious Upper Balcony member slipped the bouncer some money not to see or hear anything? If it was the woman from the entrance, Kimani felt like she could take the woman on if needed, but not if the woman had help.

Get a grip, Kimani, and stop being so paranoid.

"How about we check in on you every ten minutes?" Miguel offered.

Kimani drew in a long breath. "Okay. Let's do this."

Marissa squealed and jumped up and down. Kimani was glad she could make Marissa happy. She shouldn't let what had happened with the Scarlet Auction ruin opportunities like these.

Nevertheless, as they followed the redhead through the curtains toward the entrance where the stairs were, she couldn't shake her feeling of unease.

Chapter Thirteen

Silk upholstery on the divan and even silk wallpaper adorned the Silk Room, dimly lit with golden candelabras and wall sconces. Above the marble fireplace hung a wide life-size painting of a naked woman reclined upon a sofa. With a large bed, lavishly adorned with silk linen beneath a silk canopy, the room looked fit for a luxury bed and breakfast, and not at all what Kimani had expected to find in a BDSM club.

Weary of the bed, Kimani chose to situate herself as far from it as possible and stay near the entrance/exit. She thought once more of the woman whom she had seen go up the stairs earlier. If the woman was the one who'd invited them, was she interested in Kimani? Would the woman see and honor the white wristband or would she try to push her luck?

"May I offer you some refreshment?" the redhead asked. "We have water, soda, tea and lemonade."

"No alcohol?" Kimani asked, surprised.

"We've always been dry. Alcohol is too risky, especially in an establishment like ours."

"I respect that. I'll take a glass of water, thank you."

"Still or sparkling?"

"Still."

"We have cucumber- and blackberry-infused water, or strawberry and lemon."

"Strawberry and lemon sounds great."

After the redhead left through the curtained doorway, Kimani took a closer look at the furnishings about the room. Taking a few steps toward a dresser against the nearest wall, she opened one of the drawers, wondering why this room existed in a BDSM club.

Sure enough, her answer lie in the "jewelry" resting in velvet compartments of the first drawer: nipple clamps, collars, and gags of all kinds. Her heart skipped a beat when she saw one particularly uncomfortable-looking gag. She knew what the ball gag was like—she had worn one twice for Ben. But the one lying in the drawer beside a traditional ball gag had a metal ring with metal spokes coming out of it. It looked almost like a medical device. She picked it up and held it closer to the nearest wall sconce to study it. Maybe it wasn't intended for the mouth?

"It's a spider gag."

Her heartbeat vanished, leaving her momentarily without a pulse.

Dropping the gag into the drawer, she turned around to confirm the voice she recognized. Her heartbeat returned, palpitating quickly. It wasn't the woman she had seen earlier.

It was Ben.

He stood in partial shadow at the threshold, but

she found the whites of his eyes, and the penetration of his stare weakened her legs. Tearing herself away from his gaze, she saw that he wore a tight-fitting shirt and slim jeans that would have made her mouth water if she didn't feel trapped all of a sudden.

She shouldn't have moved away from the entry. Door or no door, it would be hard to escape.

But I was able to play him even, she recalled of their brief one-on-one basketball on the patio of his penthouse.

Nevertheless, it would be hard to get around him.

Stop being such a wuss. You're an adult. If he wants to give you a hard time, you can take it.

She squared her shoulders, a movement that did not seem to escape his notice. The guy saw everything, at least everything external.

"I take it you've never tried one," he said.

"What? That creepy-looking gag thing?" she returned, glad she could eke out a sentence without sounding too discombobulated by his presence.

"Yes. The spider gag." His voice was low and calm, devoid of emotion for now.

She shook her head. "Hell no."

"Too bad."

The redhead knocked upon the doorframe. "Your beverages."

"You can set them down," Ben replied without taking his gaze off Kimani.

The redhead entered, set the tray with the glass of water and a mug of something hot on a coffee table beside the divan, and left without further word. Silence followed until Ben held out his hand toward the divan, inviting her to sit or help herself to the water.

Kimani hesitated. The divan took her farther from the entry. But what the hell was she so afraid of? A lecture or tongue lashing for what she had done? She was prepared to own up to what had happened and apologize—two or three times if warranted. Then maybe she could finally get over him.

She walked over to the divan and picked up her glass of water. She drank it but didn't taste the infusion of strawberry and lemon. Her taste buds had somehow gone offline as her body prepared for fight or flight.

"I didn't know you were a member here," she commented when she couldn't take the silence any longer.

"That makes two of us."

"I'm not a member. I'm just...here with a friend."

His gaze dropped briefly to her wristbands. "You're not here to play?"

The question "are you?" nearly left her mouth, but she didn't want to engage in small talk. She wanted to cut to the chase and get things over with.

"I sent you a letter," she said. "I don't know if you ever got it."

"I got it."

His tone was a little cold, and she guessed her letter hadn't made much of an impact on him.

"I'm sorry," she continued, "really, really sorry. I didn't mean for the FPPC investigation to happen. I like Gordon. I'd vote for him if I could."

"And why should that matter?" There was bite in his tone.

She drew in a fortifying breath. "Look, I don't blame you if you hate me for what I did. Your uncle seems to have forgiven me—"

"I haven't."

It was a slap in the face, but it had the effect of increasing her nerve. She lifted her chin. "Why not?"

Several beats of silence passed before he said, "Maybe I don't want to. Or maybe I'm just not a forgiving guy."

She let his words sink in. Okay. She understood that. Some people required more time to forgive. Some never forgave. A part of her yearned to delve into a discussion of forgiveness, as they'd once had. But if he wasn't ready to forgive her, what was the purpose of inviting her up here?

"You spent the day walking Havenscourt."

He sauntered over slowly, she thought to take his mug of what she presumed was tea, which had been his beverage of choice for her. Green tea, to be exact. Funny how she had actually managed to acquire a taste for it after her time with Ben, even though she was far from a tea drinker. But he did nothing but stand before her. The few feet separating them felt far too short.

"I'm almost done with the precincts I have," she responded.

"You're done."

She narrowed her eyes. "What do you mean?"

"Meaning you're not walking East Oakland again."

She did a double take. "Are you running your uncle's campaign?"

He took a step closer. "As far as you're concerned, yes."

She bristled. "Does Gordon know about this? I'm a solid volunteer. And committed."

"Doesn't matter."

A lump rose in her throat. She couldn't blame him for not believing her. She probably wouldn't either if she were in his place.

"If Gordon says I can't walk East Oakland, then I won't. Otherwise, I don't see why I can't help the campaign."

He covered the distance between them as he spoke, and now was within arm's reach. His presence seemed to occupy more space than his body actually inhabited.

"You're not going to walk East Oakland because *I* say you're not. Got it, pet?"

Whoa. He did *not* just call her that. She quickly put down her glass of water, as if she needed to get ready for a boxing match.

"I'm not your pet," she replied evenly, already perturbed that he was telling her what she could or couldn't do, but she'd allowed it to pass because she understood where he was coming from. However, there was no reason to use *that term* with her.

Squaring her shoulders again, she decided it was

time for her to go. This conversation wasn't going to end well.

"I should—" she began.

But his mouth muffled the rest of her words.

Lightning bolts shot through her, the kind she got on a roller coaster—part panic, part thrill. She would have pushed away—she wasn't ready for this, hadn't asked for this—but he had some kind of kung-fu grip on her neck, holding her in a way that made her feel as if he might break her neck if she moved wrong. He tended to go for her neck, perhaps the most vulnerable part of the body, always holding her in a way that left her helpless.

So all she could do was submit to his brutal kiss. His lips crushed hers so bad, it hurt. And yet, exhilaration rushed through her. A rational dissection of what this meant—maybe he didn't hate her, maybe he was just being an asshole—would come later. For the present, she could do nothing but drown in the pressure, the heat, the excitement that was Ben.

He devoured her, his hot mouth leaving no centimeter of hers untouched, unclaimed. It was so bruising, so raw, that she almost thought he didn't know the force he used because he was drunk, but she knew Ben wouldn't drink to impairment. Something else fueled his vigor.

To her immense relief, he dropped his hold from her neck to her waist so that he could pull her to him. She slammed into his body, and the hardness at his groin snapped her to attention. She pushed against him, breaking the kiss.

He stared down at her with a look she recognized all too well, a look that said she was about to be eaten alive.

Get out while you can, Kimani.

But in addition to the scrum of emotions inside her, she was pissed. What gave him the right to kiss her like that? She wasn't his pet. She wasn't his girlfriend. She wasn't even someone he was on a date with, where an unexpected kiss might have been the result of awkward timing or miscues. Ben was the sort of guy who knew exactly what he was doing. So this was the moment for her to put him in his place. In an old-fashioned movie, this was when a woman slapped the man across the face for taking liberties. Never mind that she could probably never occupy the same room as Ben without being sexually attracted to him. If she didn't do anything or say anything, she would be condoning assault.

Oh, but being assaulted by Ben felt *so good...*

She tried pushing him away. It was a fairly weak attempt, perhaps because she knew that even if she used her whole strength, she was no match for him. The only way she could free herself is if he allowed it.

But she didn't want to be a late-night booty call because maybe that beautiful woman with him earlier hadn't been available tonight. She didn't want him thinking that he could do whatever the hell he wanted just because her body responded like crazy to him. Being trapped against him was causing arousal to swirl in her groin, growing by the second.

She glared into his dilated pupils, his eyes bright with hunger. He was waiting for her response before he pounced and moved in for the kill.

So she pounced before he could.

Throwing her arms about him, she managed to bring his head down to hers before crushing her mouth to his. Maybe it was stupid to think she could impose herself on him, the way he had on her. Maybe she was giving him exactly what he wanted. But she didn't want to be that girl seduced into submission, allowing a guy to take advantage of her indecision and ride roughshod over her reluctance. If she was going to end up on her back, it was going to be because *she* wanted it.

Even though she hated it.

She hated that she had fallen for this guy. She hated that she loved his every touch, no matter what kind it was. She hated that a part of her liked being called his pet.

Channeling her fury, she tried to bruise his lips as much as he had hers. She probably bruised her own more than anything, but she wasn't going down as a weakling.

Her ardor further ignited his. He fisted a hand through her hair, tilting her head at whatever angles suited him. But she still had moves. She shoved her hips into him. He growled as his hardness dug painfully into her belly. Their kiss became a war. Over what, she wasn't sure. Dominance, maybe. But they were each trying to prove a point.

His other hand cupped and squeezed a buttock through her jeans. She returned by threading her fingers through his short, thick hair and yanking. He grunted and bit down on her lip. She yelped, and then he was at her throat, kissing and sucking. A shaky moan escaped her lips as the siren of desire called for her to capitulate, to give in to whatever Ben wanted to do to her.

Did you forget about the chastity belt he once made you wear?

Trying to regain the offensive, she tried to pull off his shirt, wishing she could rip it as he had once done to one of her tops, though it would probably cost her half her paycheck to replace his.

But he threw her over his shoulder, walked over to the bed, and dumped her on it. Not wanting to be pinned down just yet, she tried to scramble to her knees, but he pushed her back down. The next second, he was on top of her, his mouth smothering hers.

Just once, she wanted to lead, wanted Sadie Hawkins to apply to sex, wanted to dominate him as much as he did her.

She bit down on his lip, surprising him enough for her to slip from beneath him. Pushing against his shoulders, she tried to climb on top of him, but he grabbed her around the waist and slammed her back down on the bed.

"Trying to top?" he growled. "It doesn't work that way, pet."

Her ears burned at the word. She could feel his breath heavy upon her face, his hips pressing her hard into the bed. She was going to lose a battle that had never been hers to win in the first place. The only thing she might have succeeded in doing was making him mad.

Chapter Fourteen

His pulse pounded everywhere in his body, in his bottom lip where she had bit him, and especially in his erection. Ben couldn't recall ever feeling as aroused as he did now. Every nerve inside him screamed for him to tear her clothes off and fuck her harder than he had ever fucked before. He'd fuck her through her clothes if he could.

He was a little out of breath from the kissing and her amusing little wrestling game. He liked that she was strong enough to present an interesting challenge, but she had to know she didn't stand a chance against him.

And there was no bloody way he was going to let her be the top. He had been far too lenient with her before, and he wasn't going to make that mistake again.

She glared at him, but her eyes swam with lust, and that made his cock throb even more.

"I'm not your fucking pet," she spat.

"That's too bad," he said, meeting her gaze and trying his best not to become too pulled into the depths of her large brown eyes. "Well-behaved pets get rewarded. Guess you're just going to get a fucking."

Her eyes widened, and she started shoving him, her hips bucking beneath him as if she could throw him off her body, but the motions only made his cock harder. And he would have thought he couldn't get any harder.

Damn this woman.

While his attention was fixed on the way her body brushed and pushed against his while she wriggled, she clocked him on the side of the head.

Refocusing himself, he grasped her by the throat beneath her jaw, his hand pushing up her chin. She immediately stilled.

"I'm going to give you a second chance," he told her. "I suggest you take it because there isn't going to be a third. You understand, pet?"

When she didn't respond, he squeezed her throat a little, and her hands flew to his wrist. There was no way she could pull his hand away, no way she could prevent him from breaking her neck if he were so inclined.

But he would never harm her. Punish her, yes. Scare her a little, yes. Show her who was in charge, definitely.

Her eyes said what her mouth could not because of his hold on her throat: fuck you, asshole.

It was the same look she had given him when he'd first beheld her, kneeling naked beside an equally naked Claire in Jake's cabin.

He loosened his hold a little so she could respond. "Understand?"

Despite the defiance shining in her eyes, she gave a small nod. Some men wouldn't have paused to affirm a woman's consent. They got off on being able to overpower a woman even though they knew full well biology favored testosterone in a physical struggle.

But Ben found consent from women just as sexy. Especially when a small part of them didn't actually want to. Intellectual women like Kimani could overthink things, take too many things into account, overanalyze and care too much about taking the wiser course of action. Her consent meant she couldn't resist him. It meant she wanted him. Had to acknowledge she wanted him despite her better judgment. And that sent his arousal soaring.

He pushed his pelvis into her, making her lashes flutter. He could feel her chest heaving beneath him, but he stayed his desire to pound her into oblivion.

He ran a thumb over her bottom lip before dipping into the wetness of her mouth. "So what is it my pet wants?"

She drew in several breaths and waited till he was done smearing her saliva over her lips to answer. "I want to fuck you."

Heat flared through him. He wasn't going to last long tonight, but as much as he liked her admission of desire, her choice in words wasn't lost on him. She knew the appropriate answer involved switching the subject with the object in her sentence.

He also wondered if she intended a *double-entendre*. If so, the feeling was mutual.

"And I thought you were smarter than that," he smirked.

Her eyes flashed with emotion. But she'd had her chance.

Holding her once more by the throat, he pulled her up so he could reach the candy bowl of condoms beside the bed. She tried to pull his hand away.

"You can be such a jerk sometimes."

"Is that why you get so wet for me?" he retorted.

She emitted an exasperated growl and renewed her struggles. Maybe she had changed her mind about fucking him. But it was too late now. He had to have her. Things were going to get thrashed and broken if he couldn't.

He managed to undo his belt buckle and his pants just before she kicked him in the crotch. Her foot struck him mostly on his shaft, which was so hard it could probably bulldoze a wall. He flipped her onto her stomach to limit her assault. Straddling her, he pinned her down easily despite her best efforts to buck him off.

He stripped off his shirt to release the heat burning through him. Biting on the condom wrapper, he tore it open, then rolled the condom on. The times he had gotten to take her without a condom, when they had been flesh to flesh, had been among the finest carnal experiences of his life. He wanted so much to relive that feeling, and with her pinned beneath him, he could easily do it. But while he acknowledged himself an asshole, he wasn't the kind of asshole who would take advantage of a helpless woman in that way.

It was going to be amazing being inside Kimani,

condom or not.

Laying atop her, he dry humped her a few times before fisting his hand through her hair and pulling her head up. "Still want to fuck me, babe?"

"Yes," she angrily hissed.

Coming to his knees, he reached beneath her to undo her button and zipper, then yanked her jeans and her underwear down toward her knees.

God Almighty.

It was a phrase he remembered a lady in the cafeteria at Howard liked to use. She used it whenever a male student athlete would come up to her for a third helping, if a group of students left a particularly large mess at a table, if the weather was exceptionally nice, and when the other cafeteria staff had presented her with a beautiful cake for her birthday. And Kimani's arse was better than any bloody birthday cake, better than the richest, most decadent dessert.

Lying back down, he aimed his cock beneath her arse and thrust himself into her without ceremony.

She cried out at being filled so quickly.

Bloody.

Fucking.

Hell.

She felt better than he had thought possible. He needed to lose himself in her, fast and furious. He started thrusting, too upset to see to it that she was as aroused as much as possible. Her copious wetness allowed him to sink deep, but not deep enough, given the angle of penetration. She cried out when he slammed his hips into her, his pelvis making loud smacking sounds against her arse that could probably be heard throughout the Upper Balcony.

He wasn't sure if she found the position pleasurable, but the primal had overtaken him. Anger and jealousy coursed through his blood. He wanted to punish her so badly. He wanted to drive out all thoughts of Anthony and any other guy she might partner with. He wanted to show her who was in charge, who was the Dom. He pistoned his hips, drilling her into the bed.

She turned her head to the side so that she could breathe. "Fuck! Not so hard!"

He eased his pace and ferocity. Lying still inside her, he savored the sensation of her pussy flexing about him. She wriggled her arse, trying to get some movement.

"I didn't say stop," she said

"You wanted to fuck me. Come on then."

She tried to buck against him. Feeling her wriggle again beneath him, it took all of him not to resume pounding into her. Smothered beneath his weight, her legs straight out behind her and trapped together between his thighs, she couldn't get much leverage.

After several minutes, she was huffing heavily. He liked that she wasn't a woman who expected the man to do all the work, though he was happy to do so, but he liked that Kimani wasn't afraid of a little sweat and was capable of using her muscles. But that didn't mean he was going to let her have her way.

"Ugh," she grunted. "Maybe you can get off me?"

He laughed. "Not a chance."

She tried to elbow him, but he caught her arm and bent it behind her back. He could tell she was pissed at him, but he couldn't tell if her anger was strong enough to douse her arousal. To be sure, he slid his hand beneath her pelvis to fondle her clit. She gasped. He teased the nub between her folds till it became nice and engorged.

"You should just let *me* fuck *you*," he told her. "Pet."

While holding her arm behind her back, he started moving his hips again, drawing his cock out slowly, the sinking back in slowly. He kept a languid pace, occasionally pausing as if he meant to pull out of her completely. She groaned.

Seeming to run out of patience, she said, "If you're going to fuck me, then *fuck* me."

Fuck.

With those words, there was no turning back. He slammed himself into her, but withdrew mindfully, wanting her to feel every inch of his hardness before he shoved himself back inside.

"Jesus!" she cried out before a shiver went through her.

He changed the length and rhythm of his thrusts, finding a combination that would send her over the edge. He cupped the side of her head and pushed his fingers into her mouth so that she could taste herself.

"Fuuuuuck," she wailed through his digits, just

142

before she came apart, her body jerking beneath him.

He absorbed her thrashing, which sent a new energy surging within him. He let loose and pounded into her. The creaking of the bed, the sound of flesh striking flesh, her cries muffled into the bed, were all a heady cocktail that drew his orgasm fast and strong. It blinded him. His body became waves of euphoria. His head was somewhere in the heavens.

When he settled back down, he found he had successfully withheld the ejaculation, which meant he could continue.

He had noticed her friends peeking in earlier. By their hasty retreat, he was willing to bet they would wait for Kimani to emerge rather than come get her.

After giving her a moment to recover, he withdrew and whipped his belt from his pants. He pulled her hips up while he jerked her wrists behind her thighs. He bound them together with the belt.

"Wait! What—" she protested.

He inched back so he could admire her bent form with her arse up in the air. His breath stuck in his throat as he took in her perfect ass. Smooth and unblemished, it begged to be taken. She was in the perfect position for some serious arse fucking. All he had to do was ram himself home.

Instead, he reached between her thighs. His head swam with how wet she was. After fondling her till she moaned, he brought his fingers, coated with her desire, to her lips once more. "How does my pet taste?"

At first she hesitated, but she knew what to do.

She parted her lips and allowed him to wipe his fingers on the inside of her mouth.

"I taste good," she mumbled through his fingers.

Getting off the bed, he shed his pants, then went to one of the tall dressers and opened a drawer to find a crop. Back at the bed, he said, "Your safety word is 'mercy.'"

He grabbed a buttock and dug his fingers into the luscious flesh. He massaged it, prying it from its twin so that he could see the delightful puckered hole between. Releasing the cheek, he gave it a quick smack. He tapped the crop lightly against her arse, the back of her thighs, the side of her thighs, and back up to her arse, warming her for what was to come.

"You're going to thank me after each strike," he told her. "Got that, pet?"

"How many—fuck!"

He had whipped the crop against a buttock.

"Your job is to count, pet. Nothing more. Let's try this again."

He smacked the crop to her other buttock.

"One," she muttered through gritted teeth.

"And I want a 'thank you.'"

He landed a strike across the width of her arse.

"Two. Thank you."

"A proper thank you," he said, landing an even harsher blow.

"Ow! Three. Thank you...Master."

He adjusted his crotch and took the time to marvel at her amazing backside before delivering a

144

whack that made her cry out.

"Four," she exhaled shakily. "Thank you, Master."

He brushed back the curls covering the side of her face. "Good pet. Maybe I'll reward you, after all."

Reaching beneath her rump, he gently rubbed her folds, grazing her clit every now and then. She shivered and let out a moan.

"Would you like that, pet?" he inquired as he caressed her, taking care not to attend to her clit too much, but when she didn't answer at first, he teased her sensitive pleasure bud until she did.

"Yes," she said through a shaky breath.

That's right, pet. You see, you're all mine. Mine to pleasure. To torment. To devastate.

Withdrawing his hand, we went back to spanking her with the crop. By the time he had made it to seven, his erection was ready to burst through his pants. He took in a breath to settle his ardor.

"Eight!" she squealed as the crop bit into her. "Th-Thank you, Master."

He rubbed a buttock, a rosy glow adorning it, before delivery the ninth blow. He made it to ten before throwing the crop aside. He was going to bust a nut if he waited any longer. He climbed onto the bed and knelt behind her. He slid the tip of his cock along her folds, pointing it at her slit, teasing her with a possible entry. She moaned and tried to impale herself on him, but he put a hand to her backside to keep her in place.

"Does my pet want to come again?"

"Yes," she whimpered, "Sir."

"Then beg for it."

"Please, *please* let me have your cock."

Nothing could sound more melodious than that.

"What do you want it for?" he asked, slapping her pussy lips with his member.

"I want you to fuck me with it. Please."

"Fuck you how?"

"However you want. Just do it."

"You sound like you want my cock bad. Do you, pet?"

"Yes, I want it bad."

That's right. You're gonna want mine more than anyone else's." He pushed half an inch inside her but no more.

"Please! Please fuck me."

A simple invitation, and one he couldn't refuse.

He plunged himself into her wet heat. She groaned in satisfaction. She was especially responsive in doggy style, and he was able to penetrate her better from this position.

He thrust his hand up her shirt and squeezed a tit. He pulled down the bra cup and mold the orb. She yelped when he pulled on the nipple. She had sensitive nipples, and she squeaked or gasped with every pinch and tug.

"So are you going to fuck me or what?" she asked when he reached for her other breast.

"Ask nicely."

"Please? Please fuck me."

Pulling out, he reached over and grabbed another wrapper from the candy bowl. This one contained a cock ring. After opening it, he slid the ring to the base of his shaft and turned it on. She craned her head to see the source of the vibrating sound.

"Oh my God," she exhaled when he had plunged himself back in.

Burying himself to the hilt, he sandwiched the ring between them.

"That feels gooood..."

He thrust at an even pace, making sure to grind the cock ring against her.

"Oh, yes!" she cried. "Yes!"

Grabbing her hips with both hands, he increased the pace of his thrusts. Her words devolved into grunts and groans. And then she came undone, her pussy clenched and spasmed about his cock.

He hammered himself into her to achieve his own climax. It burst through him fast and furious, this time draining through him as pleasure electrified him from head to toe. He shoved himself hard into her and milked the last of his seed from his throbbing shaft.

He did not withdraw until his cock had become flaccid enough that the condom might slip off. But he wanted to stay inside her still. Maybe for forever.

And that wasn't a good sentiment

Chapter Fifteen

"Jesus! I forgot about Marissa and Miguel!"
After Ben unbuckled the best that had bound her wrists, Kimani scrambled off the bed.

"I don't think they're too far," Ben said, grabbing his clothes off the ground.

Her eyes widened. "You saw them? Why didn't you tell me?"

It was a pointless question because what was done was done. Sheshimmied up her underwear and pants. Ugh. Nothing like having to pull up wet and squishy clothing.

She turned to leave, but he grabbed her arm.

"Kimani," he'd said.

Unable to read the emotions in his eyes, she tore herself away. "I shouldn't keep them waiting."

Stumbling out of the Silk room, she found Marissa and Miguel sitting on a sofa down the hallway.

"Where were you guys?" she asked.

"Well, we did look in on you," Marissa replied, getting to her feet, "but you were kind of busy."

Kimani flushed to the roots of her hair. In truth, she had forgotten about Marissa and Miguel.

Marissa leaned in and lowered her voice. "Hey, he was totally hot. I'd jump him, too."

After they said goodbye to Miguel and were in the

backseat of a taxi headed home, Marissa pounced. "So, who was he?"

It was the question Kimani dreaded. Looking out the window of the taxi, she drew in a breath. "A guy I met when I went undercover."

"No shit! Did he bid on you at the Scarlet Auction?"

"He didn't participate in the auction. Exactly."

"Then how'd you meet him?"

"He was an acquaintance of a guy who *did* do the auction."

"What's his name?"

"Ben."

"That's all you're going to give me? He must be loaded if he's friends with people who can afford the Scarlet Auction. Maybe that's why he gets to be a member of the Upper Balcony."

Now that she had room to think about and regret what had happened between her and Ben, Kimani couldn't resist feeling a little irritated. "And if he does have money, what does that matter?"

"Just saying. I mean, if he's good-looking and rich, you totally scored."

"There are plenty of good-looking, rich, and powerful men who are nothing but misogynists and criminals. And they get to get away with shit because of their looks, their wealth or their status in society."

"I just assumed that your guy wasn't one of *those* guys because Kimani Taylor doesn't drop her pants for *those* guys. Am I right?"

Kimani sighed. "I'm sorry. I didn't mean to get bitchy. He's not *my* guy, you know. You should have seen the gorgeous woman he was with earlier today."

"Wait, you saw him already today?"

"It was a chance encounter."

"And he knew you were coming to The Lair?"

"He couldn't have. I didn't mention The Lair."

"It's quite the coincidence."

Kimani shrugged. Sometimes life was stranger than fiction.

"So, he must have seen you from the Upper Balcony, and you're the reason we got invited up there."

"I guess."

"He must really be into you."

Kimani sat with the idea for a moment, wishing that what Marissa had said was true, then deciding it was better if it wasn't. "I don't think so. We had some unresolved issues. That's what the, um, sex was about."

"Hm. Guess that's one to add to the list next to make-up sex and rebound sex: 'unresolved-issues' sex. Did you resolve your issues?"

At that, Kimani had to laugh. "No."

We could have made them worse, she thought to herself.

"Does that mean you guys will have to have sex again?"

"No!"

Her vociferousness took Marissa by surprise. "Why not? If I had a guy like that, I'd try to resolve the

150

issues over and over again. And then one or two more times just for good measure."

"How much did you and Miguel witness?"

"Well, we saw you grab him and kiss him. Then we went exploring the rest of the Upper Balcony. We came across the Dungeon Room and checked out all the different implements they had. Then we came back, and I peeked in on you. There's something about your guy—"

"You can call him Ben."

"Right. There's something about him, the way he moves, the way he was holding you and pounding you from behind that was, like, incredibly hot."

Kimani blushed. "Then what did you and Miguel do?"

"We sat down and decided to wait for you to be done. We talked a lot."

"Miguel seems like a really nice guy."

"He is. There were a few times in the Dungeon Room when I could tell he was getting turned on and probably would've been open to doing something, but he didn't say anything. It was like he knew I wasn't ready, even though I never told anyone why I haven't played in a while."

"That's cool."

"He said we was planning to go to The Lair next Friday. I told him I might go then, too, depending on my work schedule."

Kimani was able to turn the conversation toward the topic of Miguel, which Marissa seemed happy to talk about, and which used up the rest of the ride so there was no time to go back to talking about Ben. Once inside their home, Kimani professed to being really tired.

"I'll bet you're tired," Marissa teased. "Maybe we should go back to The Lair together next Friday. Maybe your guy—I mean, Ben—will invite us up to the Upper Balcony again."

"I wouldn't be surprised if I never hear from him again," Kimani said.

"Really?"

"Yeah, I think he just needed to get his money's worth, so to speak."

"So he's like a use-'em-then-leave-'em kind of guy?"

"I don't think he's relationship material." But even as she said it, she wondered how true that was. She had been too quick to judge him before. "And even if he was, he wouldn't be looking for a relationship with me."

"How can you be so sure?"

"Gut feeling."

"Well, good thing you don't need to be in a relationship to enjoy The Lair!"

Kimani smiled, briefly entertaining the idea that she and Ben could be BDSM partners. However, given the feelings she already had for Ben, keeping things to just sex would be easier said than done.

*****

Though running late, Kimani headed to the *Tribune* offices in relatively high spirits. She had met with Gordon and pitched her idea to do an event in East Oakland, and he had agreed to it. She could hardly wait to get started on organizing some three-on-three games to make the event more fun. It would take a lot of work to pull it off in just two weeks' time, but she was excited.

At her request, she and Gordon had met at a tea shop, away his from campaign headquarters so that she wouldn't run into Ben. A part of her hoped she would never see him again. Given how raw and roughed up he had left her body, she wondered how she had even made it home. Thirty-six hours later, she was still faintly sore between the legs.

She wondered what he had intended to say to her just before she'd exited the Silk Room, and she wished she had stayed a minute longer to find out, but whatever it was, it couldn't have been that important or he would have found a way to contact her. He knew she worked for the *Tribune,* but when she went to her desk, she saw that she had no new voicemails.

She went over to Sam's office to talk about the possibility of Robin covering the event she was organizing for Gordon.

"We can cover it, but I'm afraid we won't be able to print it," he replied with a heavy sigh.

She did a double take. "Why not?"

Sam sighed again. "I just got a call from the lawyer representing the new owner. They're shutting us down, effective immediately."

"What?! Why?"

"He didn't say. We're going to get paid as if the paper was still up and running, but there won't be a newspaper for tomorrow."

She took a seat in front of Sam's desk as she tried to process the information. "This doesn't make much sense. What's the urgency, especially if they're keeping us on payroll?"

Sam shook his head, apparently equally as puzzled. "My guess is still that the new owners, New Western Media, is linked somehow to a rival news outlet, and they bought us to get rid of the competition even though our readership has been shrinking, and, the way things were going, we might have died a more natural death, so to speak."

"So New Western Media is in some kind of hurry. Is there any way to talk to them?"

"Only through their attorney, Murray Jones. I tried to find out more information about New Western, but all I could dig up was their LLC filings with the Secretary of State. No owners listed, only the law firm of Jones and Finch, LLP, is listed as the agent of representation. The LLC is newly formed, probably for the sole purpose of acquiring the *Tribune*."

"They won't even let us print a final paper? A goodbye issue? What about the readers who have subscribed and paid for the paper?"

"I'm guessing they'll get refunds. If New Western Media can afford to pay us to do nothing, they can probably afford to prorate the subscriptions."

Kimani still couldn't wrap her head around the strangeness of the acquisition. She thought about the profile of Gordon. Robin had showed her a draft, and it was shaping up nicely.

"So what do we do with all the stories we're currently working on?" she asked Sam. "Do you think we could sell them to..."

But Sam was shaking his head. "We're to cease and desist all activities and pack up our things today. They're going to lock the offices at midnight tonight."

"Jesus."

"I need a few minutes before I make the announcement on the floor. Drinks on me tonight."

They sat in silence for a few moments.

"I knew my stint here might not last long," Kimani said at last, "and though I didn't think it would end like this, I'm grateful for each day I was here and thankful for the opportunity you gave me."

Sam returned a wan smile. "I'm sorry it didn't turn out."

"Don't be sorry. I appreciate your support of me. And it was fun while it lasted."

"Well, I hope you find something else that's fun while job hunting."

"You should find something fun, too."

"I think I'll take that camping trip to Yosemite that my husband has been bugging me to do."

"I've never been, but Yosemite looks beautiful."

She got up to give Sam the time he needed to gather his thoughts and what he wanted to say to the staff.

Everyone else was as shocked as she was to hear the news. Most were dedicated journalists who would have happily worked instead of getting paid to do nothing.

"Guess I'll go back to doing wedding photography for a bit," said Ron, as he, Kimani and Robin ate lunch at a nearby bakery.

"I wish happy hour started now," said Robin.

They at their lunch of soup and sandwiches in relative quiet.

"You guys go on ahead," Kimani said when they were done. "I want to order an iced tea to go."

As she ordered, she marveled that she chose an iced *green* tea. She had fully acquired the taste for green tea now.

Upon exiting, she heard a voice that sent chills through her bones.

"Well, well, well. If it isn't Slut #2."

She decided to keep walking until he said, "What? Not even a 'hello' to your Master?"

She whipped around and met the bright blue eyes of Jake Whitehurst. Except for the stubble, he looked exactly as he had during their time together: a Ken doll with his good looks and soft golden hair. Too bad they masked a complete SOB.

"You're not supposed to come within a hundred

yards of me or you're in violation of the restraining order," she told him.

He smirked. "Hey, not my fault we happened to want to get coffee from the same place."

She turned to walk away but stopped once more when he spoke.

"Funny how you're a reporter. I'm guessing you didn't tell the people at the Scarlet Auction about that."

She met his gaze again, and despite his cool demeanor, she saw the hate simmering in his eyes.

How did he know she was a reporter? She supposed it wouldn't be hard to discover. All he had to do was see her name in the byline of a *Tribune* article, and though she had used a fake name while participating in the Scarlet Auction, her real name was revealed when she pressed charges against him.

Was he somehow connected with New Western Media? Was he behind the acquisition and shutdown? Somehow, though she knew Jake to be well off, she doubted he had the wherewithal and the assets to purchase the *Tribune*. But if he knew she worked for the *Tribune*, he would probably have loved to put her out of a job. But the generosity of the severance package didn't sound like something Jake would do.

"What's it to you?" she asked, to see if he would say anything that would connect him to New Western Media.

His eyes narrowed. "Was Benji boy in on your little charade?"

He had touched a raw chord, and, deciding it wasn't worth it—whether or not Jake was involved with the shutdown of the *Tribune* probably wouldn't change the outcome—she turned away.

"I bet he was. Since he's such a pussy for black cunt."

Turning back around, she gave Jake a hard stare. "You're deliberately violating the restraining order."

"Sluts like you need a real Dom. They need to be put in their place. You know there's nothing society hates more than an obnoxious, big-lipped black woman with a mouth on her. I'd put that mouth to proper use."

Her cheeks burned.

Don't get into it. It's not worth it. He's baiting you. Maybe he's hoping to press assault charges on you.

But she wanted nothing more than to throw her tea at him. Restraining herself, she instead reached for her phone to call the police.

Before she could swipe her phone open, however, Jake grabbed her hand, squeezing so hard she dropped her phone.

"Calling for your pussy boy?" he sneered.

"Ma'am, this guy bothering you?" a stranger asked.

Even though there were plenty of people walking about, and a woman exiting the bakery earlier had lifted her brow when Jake was talking, Kimani was relieved that someone had intervened.

Jake took in the size and obvious strength of the

man, and dropped Kimani's hand. Without a word, he stalked away. The stranger picked up Kimani's phone.

"Thanks," she said, receiving her phone back.

The man gave a curt nod and continued on his way. Though rattled by the incident, Kimani called the police to report the violation of the restraining order.

It wasn't until she was back in her office and had time to fully settle her nerves that she realized the stranger looked and sounded familiar. He had on reflective sunglasses, so she couldn't see his eyes, but he reminded her of the man with the coughing fit outside her place the night of the break-in.

Chapter Sixteen

Ben's whole body tightened. "He fucking touched her?"

"He grabbed her hand," Moe, on the other end of the call, confirmed.

Ben looked out his office window at the Bay Bridge, fixing his attention on the structure to calm himself. He could kill the bloody wanker. What the hell was that motherfucker up to?

"Did she inform the authorities that Jake was in violation of his restraining order?" Ben asked.

"She made a call after the incident, but I couldn't get close enough to hear what it was," Moe replied. "I didn't want her to notice me and wonder why I was hanging around."

"How did she look afterward?"

"Shaken up a little but otherwise okay."

Fucking Jake Whitehurst. After finishing with Moe, Ben called Bataar.

"You want daily reports on Jake," Bataar guessed before Ben had said anything.

"I don't want the fucker anywhere near Kimani," Ben said. "Make sure your guys are in communication with each other so that what happened today doesn't happen again. The dipshit knows he can't touch me, so he's going after her instead."

"I'm on it, boss."

Ben hung up, but he didn't feel mollified. Part of him wanted to confront Jake, even let the wanker come at him if it meant he would leave Kimani alone. He could threaten Jake, but that would only make Jake more passive-aggressive, and that kind of blustering and chest thumping was for men whose brains weren't large enough to command their penises.

The screen on his desk phone indicated he had an incoming call from the Dean of the Stanford Graduate School of Business. Ben let it go to voicemail so that he could continue his thoughts on Jake. He had never like the guy, but unlike Kimani, he'd underestimated what Jake was capable of. What was it going to take to get the guy to leave Kimani alone?

Leaning back in his chair, Ben closed his eyes to slow the swirl of thoughts and emotions. Bumping into Kimani had kicked up a sandstorm of conflicting desires.

It had not been an easy weekend.

After deciding he was going to The Lair, he had told Eumie he was going to put her up at a hotel or, if she wanted, he would fly her back to Hong Kong.

She had not received it well.

"What's the matter with you men?" she'd asked while she threw her things into her suitcase. "I thought we had a nice arrangement, but too much sex and you freak out that we're in a relationship?"

He didn't say anything. It was better she believed that than the real reason he didn't want her around anymore.

But even if she wasn't especially astute, she had a woman's intuition.

"Or is it someone else?" she had realized, narrowing her eyes at him. "You planning to go pussy-hopping?"

"None of your business if I did," he replied.

"Who is she? Don't tell me it's that black girl I saw you talking to today? Does your father know you're banging a black person?"

"I don't care what my father does or doesn't know."

She had given him a look of disgust, and he'd left her to finish packing on her own.

He hadn't planned on having sex with Kimani when he'd arrived at The Lair, but he'd known he wanted to. The thought of her submitting to another man was too much.

She. Was. His.

The sex hadn't satiated him at all. He wanted more. He wanted to keep her.

When he had stopped her from leaving at first, he had been tempted to say something to that effect. But the moment had passed, and he had allowed it to. He didn't want to be rash. While pounding into her had been cathartic and diffused his anger, it had only amplified his desire for her. And knowing, seeing, smelling, hearing her responding to him, wanting him as much as he wanted her, was the headiest aphrodisiac.

I want to fuck you.

While he had insisted on being the one doing the fucking, no words had ever sounded hotter or sexier. There was so much more he wanted to do to her. If he'd had the whole week with her that he'd paid for...it still wouldn't have been enough.

The desk phone beeped, indicating he had a new voicemail message. Opening his eyes, he glanced at the screen to see the transcription. The dean had tickets to an upcoming Stanford football game, 50-yard line, and was offering them to Ben, whom he was soliciting for an endowment for a new faculty position.

Ben immediately thought of Kimani. She hadn't mentioned if she liked football, but he imagined she might, imagined how her eyes might light up if he invited her to the game.

It would be a date. Though their evening at Ishikawa West had looked like a date, they had had to have dinner somewhere, so why not a Michelin three-star restaurant? But a football game would say something different.

Picking up the phone, he decided to call the dean back to accept the tickets.

*****

Several days passed and Ben hadn't heard from Kimani. He knew she wasn't the sort to play games, the kind that Eumie would, the I'm-going-to-wait-until-he-calls-me-first-so-it-feels-like-I'm-hard-to-get moves that made dating feel like a game of chess.

Fuck chess.

"Women play those types of games because they work," May had explained to him once. "Not all the time. But enough times that they've lasted the centuries. Besides, men play similar games in the realm of business and politics."

But Ben usually just took what he wanted, and he didn't like to do business with people who played coy. With Kimani, he sure as hell knew what he wanted— her, pinned beneath him a million different ways.

He hadn't reached out to her, however, because it seemed, based on her haste to leave that night at The Lair, that she needed some space. Probably to convince herself that being his fucktoy was far from wise. But if that was her conclusion, he wasn't worried. He'd have her wet and whimpering again.

From Bill, Ben found out that Kimani was headed to the campaign headquarters. After having had to clean out her desk earlier in the week, Ben suspected she would need a little cheering up, and he hoped the pair of football tickets might do it.

"I'll take those precincts," she was saying to Anthony, pointing to the folders for the area of Lockwood Gardens.

Anthony, spotting Ben standing behind her, hesitated and responded, "I have some other precincts that could use a second pass."

"Has Lockwood Gardens even had a first pass?"

"No, but it wouldn't be wise to walk these

precincts alone, and I don't know that we have a volunteer who can go with you right now."

"I'll find a friend."

Anthony furrowed his brow. "I don't know..."

Irritated that Anthony wasn't able to put down his foot harder, Ben stepped in. "You have a death wish?" he asked Kimani.

Not realizing he had been behind her, she jumped back in surprise. She was casually dressed in a zip-up hoodie and shorts. She looked so hot, he wanted to rip the clothes off and take her right there.

"Excuse me?" she returned.

"I said you're done walking East Oakland," he replied.

"There are other East Oakland neighborhoods, not the flats, of course—" Anthony began, till Ben gave him a cutting look.

"Fine," she huffed. "I'll take whatever you want to give me."

Relieved, Anthony handed her a set of folders and the doorhangers. She received them and headed out. Ben followed.

"Don't get any ideas about using those doorhangers in Lockwood Gardens," he said.

She flushed with guilt and pressed her lips together in an unhappy line. She turned to face him. "What do you want?"

To devastate you.

His gaze spoke the words, and she seemed to find it difficult to swallow. They could have spent a while staring at each other, but he released her from his stare to call Bataar to bring the car around.

"Are you planning to walk now?" he asked her.

"I was."

"Then I'll give you a lift."

She hesitated, but there was no reason on the surface for her not to accept his offer. They got in the backseat of his Porsche. Of course, all he wanted to do was reach over and molest her, but he behaved. He knew she got self-conscious with Bataar around. Which made it all the more fun to try to get her aroused, but he decided not to torment her...for the moment.

"You can drop me off here," she said to Bataar, indicating the intersection of two streets on the map in her folder.

Anthony had given her a precinct in the hills of East Oakland of solid working-class neighborhoods. Bataar parked in front of a row of shoebox homes built in the '50s. Ben noticed a black Honda pull up on the cross street. Probably Bill.

Kimani hopped out, looking relieved to be out of the car. Her relief was short-lived when she saw that he had gotten out as well. Overdressed for the occasion, he removed his jacket and placed it in the backseat. He saw Kimani's gaze sweep over his short-sleeve shirt, fitted enough to hint at the muscles beneath.

He held out his hand. "Give me the other side of the street."

"You're walking, too?" she asked.

"Why not? The candidate is my uncle."

Despite that fact, he had not walked a precinct yet. His focus had been to raise money for the campaign.

She handed him the voter list with the odd-numbered houses while she kept the list with the even numbers. She then handed him some doorhangers.

"I'm guessing we're supposed to talk to the voters who haven't been identified as voting for Gordon or the other candidates," she explained, looking over the lists. She laid out a plan for how they could cover the precinct with minimal overlap of walking.

It was the perfect day for precinct walking. Sunny but not overly warm. It was hard to beat autumn weather in the Bay Area, especially in the East Bay, which tended to be sunnier and warmer than the city.

Ben would have preferred to walk with Kimani, but this was about helping Uncle Gordon. However, he found he enjoyed looking at her from across the street, seeing her smile as she greeted a resident and hearing her enthusiasm as she talked about why Gordon would make a great mayor.

"I'll have Bataar bring us some lunch," he said to her after they had been walking for two hours. "What would you like?"

"Whatever you feel like getting," she replied.

She sounded cheerful and relaxed, perhaps feeling safe that he wouldn't try anything in broad daylight. She was wrong, of course, but he liked her current mood too much to mess with it. For now.

After walking another hour, they took a break for lunch. Bataar had returned with Korean rice bowls. They sat down on the sidewalk. Bataar had already eaten and chose to sit in the car.

"What is this?" Kimani asked, poking at the cabbage with red sauce with her chopsticks. She had gone back to her old way of holding the utensil.

"Kimchi," he answered. "It's an amazing food. Full of probiotics."

She wrinkled her nose. "Are you going to make me eat it?"

"Don't tempt me," he replied as he tried to focus on the food.

She flushed, and clearly decided it was best she took the initiative to try the kimchi.

"Okay, not great, but not bad," she deemed. "Crunchy and soggy at the same time. I like that it's spicy."

And he liked that she wasn't completely adverse to trying new things, including the raw egg that he'd had for breakfast their first morning at his place in Pacific Heights. Eumie would have rolled her eyes and gagged at the thought.

Noticing that she struggled with scooping up the rice with her chopsticks, he wrapped an arm around her and placed his hand on hers to show her a better grip.

"Anchor the bottom stick so that it doesn't move," he explained. "You'll get much better leverage that way."

Her fingers slipped, sending grains of rice flying into his face.

"Jesus, I'm sorry," she giggled.

He stared at her. Her smile. The brightness of her eyes. Her laugh.

I want to fuck you so bad right now.

She seemed to know his thoughts, and tried to dispel the mood by asking, "How long did it take you to get the hang of using chopsticks?"

"Hard to say," he answered, picking the rice off his shirt. "I've probably been using them since I was two years old."

She brightened. "I wonder what you were like at two years old?"

"Difficult. My older sister wasn't too keen on me. She said I was always pulling her hair, and my mother said I cried a lot. Supposedly she tried to work from home but couldn't get anything done."

"What does your mom do?"

"She's a professor of economics."

"You come from an accomplished family."

"Which is good and bad. It's what I rebelled against as a kid."

"So how come you got it together?"

Ben leaned back on his arms and thought. "I grew up. And my time at Howard made a difference. As a freshman, I used to get into the most heated debates. I was advantaged but didn't see myself as that different. But learning the history of a people repressed for centuries in the worst ways made me grateful for what I have. And Uncle Gordon. During my time at college, he was basically a father to me."

He looked over at her. "And what was two-year-old Kimani like?"

"Also difficult. My mother said I was constantly trying to climb things, and I liked to throw things. Just for fun."

She flicked her chopsticks, and more rice came his way.

"You did that on purpose," he said.

She returned a guilty smile, but her smile turned into a gasp when he pulled her by the neck toward him. His mouth brushed against her curls as he said into her ear, "Keep that up, and I'll do you right here against the car."

"Families with kids live in these houses," she hissed.

"Then I'll throw you in the backseat of the car."

Her lashes fluttered, and despite the tenseness in her body, the pupils in her eyes had dilated. His gaze fell to her lips. He knew what he really wanted for lunch. And the vision of her squirming beneath him in the confines of the car was very, very appealing.

He took her mouth. Not in the bruising way he had in the Silk Room. This kiss was about savoring. He tasted the suppleness of her lips, the heat of her mouth, the texture of her tongue. Different emotions flavored this kiss, though he knew it wouldn't be long before more primal, visceral urges took over.

She put her hand on his wrist and—reluctantly, it seemed—pulled away.

"We should finish the precinct," she said, breathlessly.

He could wipe away her resistance with another demanding kiss, he was sure of it. But he needed to show her—and himself—that he possessed control. He would behave.

For now.

Chapter Seventeen

When they arrived back at the campaign headquarters, Ben went to talk with his uncle and aunt. Since Kimani hadn't yet had a chance to replace her stolen laptop, she sat at one of the computers in the headquarters to print out more flyers for the Havenscourt basketball event. She had secured a nonprofit partner, East Oakland Kids, that would accept the funds raised and spearhead the improvements to the basketball courts.

"Hi," a sultry voice behind her said. "We didn't get to meet the other day."

Turning around, Kimani found herself staring at a stunning statuesque woman of Chinese descent, supremely slender except for her breasts, which were pushed by her underwire bra into a significant cleavage above a scoop neck top. Kimani instantly remembered her. The woman had been in the company of Alice Lee, and Kimani had picked up a connection between her and Ben—a connection that suggested the two weren't just friends.

"You left rather suddenly," the woman said, arching perfectly tweezed brows.

Kimani got to her feet and held out her hand. "Hi. I'm Kimani Taylor."

"Eu-meh Ma. But you can call me Eumie. I'm the

other woman that Ben's banging."

Taken aback, Kimani didn't know what to say at first. "...Excuse me?"

Eumie tossed her long black hair to the side. "That Benjamin Lee. He's such a manwhore, isn't he?"

"Is he?"

"Sometimes I wonder why we put up with him? I bet he has a white girl, maybe even a *Mexican* girl he's banging, too." Eumie shivered as if a plate of creepy crawlers had been placed before her for breakfast. "Like he's the fucking United Nations with sex."

The wiser part of Kimani told her she should just cut the conversation short, but the emotional part of her wouldn't let her leave. Like driving by a traffic accident, she couldn't resist sparing a glance. Did this woman have a purpose in initiating this conversation or was she just making small talk and usually this candid?

"But, you know, he's not even that great sometimes," Eumie continued. "The other night, he just gave up and took the easy way out by making me use a vibrator. Maybe he's getting old and losing his stamina."

Okay, now is a good time to exit the conversation.

"I'm sorry to have to be short—it was nice meeting you—but I should get these flyers printed," Kimani said, hitting the print button and heading over to the printer.

Eumie followed her. "Oh, are you working for Uncle Gordon?"

"I'm a volunteer. Are you family?"

"Alice Lee is a cousin of mine. Ben suggested I come and visit her and Gordon. When he invited me to fly out here with him, I thought, why not? I haven't seen Alice in a long time."

Kimani couldn't stop a small pit from opening in her stomach. She supposed she shouldn't be surprised that Ben was sleeping around. What she had with Ben didn't qualify as a relationship. But somehow it had felt *different* when they were precinct walking together in East Oakland.

She gave a silent sigh. Maybe it had been her imagination.

"Although I wasn't sure it was such a good idea at first," Eumie said. "I thought he might want to get back together again since we used to date, but I did not want to revive our old relationship. He was so bossy and possessive. The worst boyfriend material. So I'm very relieved to find he's screwing someone else at the same time."

Was she? Kimani thought she heard a hint of sarcasm.

"Because I'm focused on my modeling career. What is it that you do?"

"I'm a news reporter," Kimani answered. "For the *San Francisco Tribune*. Or, I was."

"Oh, is that the thing that Ben recently bought?"

The small pit in her stomach suddenly opened into a chasm. "What?"

"How funny...I overhead him talking to his

attorney or someone like that about shutting down a paper with the word *Tribune* in it. But I was in Ben's shower, so I didn't catch everything that was said. So is it just a coincidence that he's having sex with you?"

Kimani looked past Eumie to Gordon's office. Ben was still talking to his uncle and aunt, but, as if he sensed that she was looking his way, he turned. He stiffened. Most likely because he had noticed Eumie. It was probably a guy's worst nightmare to find his ex-girlfriends talking together. No, Eumie was the only ex-girlfriend.

I'm just a fucktoy. A fucktoy he put out of a job.

Chapter Eighteen

Ben didn't need to hear what Eumie said to know that it wasn't good. Excusing himself, he exited Gordon's office and made straight for Eumie and Kimani. The look on Kimani's face confirmed his suspicions. What the hell had Eumie said?

"Oh, hi, Benji," Eumie greeted when she heard him behind her. She turned back to Kimani. "Do you call him Benji, too, or does he have a different pet name with you?"

Kimani's frown deepened.

"Eumie," he said in a tone one would use with a wayward child.

"Kim-hani and I were just exchanging notes," she replied with a devilish grin.

He looked to Kimani, who stared at him with more intensity than he had ever seen from her.

"Is your attorney a man by the name of Murray Jones?" she asked, her voice quivering slightly.

"I have a lot of attorneys," he answered. "He's one of them. Why?"

She glanced at Eumie before returning her gaze to him.

Her bottom lip trembled. Her eyes narrowed. "So it's true. It was *you*."

He looked at Eumie. Had Eumie told Kimani

about his acquisition of the *Tribune*? But how would Eumie have known? He suddenly remembered their last night together: he had left his bathroom door open, Eumie was showering, and...shit.

Sensing a storm, Eumie decided to seek safer grounds. "I should go see if Aunt Alice is ready. We're going to see a movie. The new one by—well, I should check on her."

He barely noticed Eumie leaving. His gaze was on Kimani, and the emotion on her face was like a knife to his gut.

"Why—" he began.

"I don't know why I didn't... Jesus, I can't believe you would do such a thing!" Kimani exploded.

Before he jumped to conclusions, he asked in a steady voice, though his pulse had quickened, "What are you referring to?"

"You! You bought the *Tribune* and shut it down."

She stared at him as if challenging him to deny it.

"I did," he acknowledged.

"That—that's so wrong!"

"What was *wrong* was the *Tribune* running that article suggesting the independent expenditure was connected to Uncle Gordon."

"Okay, that article was premature, but it contained only facts. In a way, the IE was connected to your uncle through you."

"I removed myself from the IE before it was officially formed. The way those 'facts' in that article were laid out made it seem Uncle Gordon and I were doing something unlawful. And you know that."

"That's no reason to shut down a good paper—out of *revenge*."

"I'm trying to protect Uncle Gordon. That piece you're working on now about him—"

"It's supposed to *help* Gordon! My editor wasn't even sure he wanted to run it because it wasn't hard-hitting enough."

"How can you be sure that the article will be favorable? What if you guys end up doing more damage?"

"So you're going to try to control the press?"

"If you're upset about losing your job, I'll—"

"It's not just about *me*! You put a lot of good people out of work."

"What do you want? A larger severance for everyone?"

"Look, I don't know what it's like in China, but a free press is vital to democracy. And it's getting harder and harder for quality journalism to survive."

"Frankly, that's not my problem."

Shit. He shouldn't have said that.

She stared at him in silence, her chest rising and falling with large breaths.

He drew in his own breath to lower his blood pressure. "I'll extend the salaries of everyone—"

"You can do that, but I'm not going to take your money. I don't *want* your money."

She grabbed papers off the printer and stuffed them into her handbag.

Fuck. She was pissed. He didn't want her upset, but his own anger hadn't dissipated.

"Kimani, I'm sorry that—"

She shook her head as she shouldered her handbag. "I don't want to hear it."

She started walking out of the headquarters. He matched her quick strides. "What I did...you might have considered doing the same if you were in my place."

She glared at him. "No, I wouldn't. I wouldn't have shut down a legitimate newspaper just because I could. I wouldn't have paid two hundred thousand dollars to have sex with someone for a week. Just because you *can* doesn't mean you *should*!"

He grabbed her arm and stopped her. "Would you rather I'd left you with Jake Whitehurst?"

"That wasn't the point I was making."

She yanked herself free and was out the door. Exactly where she was headed, he couldn't tell.

"The point you're making is that you're a better person," he said. "Fine. I won't deny I'm an asshole, but all's fair in love and war, love."

"That is a bogus cliché to excuse men from playing less than fair."

"Fair? You want to talk fair? How is an FPPC investigation into an innocent man fair?"

She pursed her lips. "I'm sorry that happened. I'm sorry in so many ways, there's probably not *enough* ways for me to say it. So I guess we're even now."

They were in front of a bus stop.

"I'll take you home," he said.

"I don't want you to take me home."

She looked down the street. There was no bus in sight. Spotting a man standing next to his car, she hurried toward him. "Excuse me, sir, would you mind giving me a lift?"

Bill glanced at Ben, clearly taken by surprise. "Well, um..."

"I'll pay you fifty bucks," she offered.

"You don't need a ride," Ben intervened. "Bataar can—"

She whirled around to face him. "I don't want a ride from you. I don't want to be with you right now!"

"So you're going to get a ride from a total stranger?" he demanded.

"I've got my cellphone, I'll be fine," she responded through gritted teeth. "And, frankly, I'm not your problem."

Without waiting for Bill to respond, she opened the passenger door and hopped in. Bill looked awkwardly at Ben but fished out his keys.

Fuck! He didn't want to let her go, but he couldn't think of anything to say to convince her to stay. Maybe she would be better off with some time and distance to cool off. He gave Bill a nod.

Bill got in the car. "Where do you need to go, miss?"

Ben watched them drive away. He could total a car right now. Drive his fist into a streetlight. Instead, he only stood on the sidewalk as conflicting emotions raged inside him. Part of him was tormented by her anger and dismay and only wanted to make things right for her. Another part of him was incensed that she couldn't see his side of things. Sure, saying that the shutdown of her newspaper wasn't his problem sounded harsh, but it was the truth. And the *Tribune* wouldn't have lasted long anyway.

But knowing that didn't make him feel better.

Turning around, he walked back toward his car. Bataar, leaning against the Porsche and soaking in the warm California sun, straightened. Seeing that his boss was unhappy, Bataar didn't say a word. It was one of the better qualities in men. A woman would pounce with questions like "What's wrong?" and "Is everything okay?"

It was fucking obvious that things were far from okay. And he hadn't even had the chance to ask Kimani about the football game.

Chapter Nineteen

Kimani hit the decline button on her cell when Ben's number came up. How many times had she tried calling him? Now the shoe was on the other foot. She didn't refuse his calls because she was into payback. She didn't want to talk to him because she was too heartbroken. In a way, the closure of the *Tribune* was her fault. If she had never told Sam about that text that led to the article that led to Ben's anger, the *Tribune* might still be up and running.

She looked herself over in the mirror to make sure she looked good in her slim trouser pants, blouse and blazer. A local lifestyle magazine was looking for a part-time writer, and though the job included some marketing duties and was far from ideal, Kimani wanted work. She could keep herself busy with Gordon's campaign, but the more she worked for Gordon, the more she increased her chances of running into Ben.

She noticed he hadn't left a voicemail this time. His previous two messages had been short, mostly asking her to call him back. A part of her was surprised he bothered calling her...as if he cared.

After seeing that her hair was in order and noticing that the taxi cab was outside, she grabbed her cell, handbag and portfolio. Stepping out of her house, she nearly jumped out of her skin.

"Jesus! What are you doing here?" she asked Ben.

He stood within arm's reach of her, looking amazingly sexy in a simply slim-fit Henley and jeans. He wore the Louis Vuitton sunglasses he had let her borrow while on Jake's boat.

"You wouldn't pick up my calls," he explained.

"I didn't feel like talking to you," she replied and made a move to indicate she wanted to pass.

He didn't budge.

"Kimani, I'm sorry."

She took in a deep breath. He sounded sincere, and she rather suspected that apologies were not something he said often. But was it enough to absolve him of what he had done?

"I've already told Murray to increase the severance package for everyone," he continued. "It'll be a sliding scale after three months, but you'll have up to six months of pay with full health benefits."

"That's very generous, Ben, but you can't buy your way into everything."

He seemed taken aback. "Do you know that when I bought the *Tribune*, the owners weren't going to keep it open past three months? Now you get full pay without even having to go to work."

"And if the *Tribune* wasn't struggling? Would you still have purchased it?"

"Yes."

"All because of that one article we ran?"

"That article could cost him the election in the

end. I need to make it right for Uncle Gordon."

Hearing the pain in his voice, a part of her wanted to comfort him, to tell him that it wasn't his fault. But she wasn't ready to forgive him.

"Does your uncle know what you did?" she asked him.

"No. I haven't told him because he doesn't have to know."

"And because he wouldn't have approved of what you're doing!"

"I would have done what I did with or without Uncle Gordon's approval."

Kimani shook her head and tried to walk past him, but he caught her by the arm.

"Kimani, I'm sorry that you don't have a job at the *Tribune* anymore. If there's anything I can—"

"Oh, no, you've done enough. In fact, I have an interview to get to. So unless you want to make me late..."

Reluctantly, he let her go. "I'll give you a ride to your interview."

"I don't want a ride or anything else from you."

The words came out more sharply than she intended, but she was able to walk away and get into the taxi. After telling the driver her destination, she settled back into the seat and almost felt like crying. Had she done the right thing? Should she have been more forgiving? Did it matter?

The questions occupied her right up to the interview, which didn't go as well as Kimani would have liked, so she wasn't surprised when the magazine called her the next day and told her they were going to go with someone else.

*****

The rest of the week, Kimani channeled her anger and misery into organizing the community event for Gordon. She had sent press releases to the media, gotten local grocery stores to donate bottled water, and coordinated with Gordon's campaign staff to supply snacks and volunteers to take donations. The event was looking good.

She only hoped that Ben didn't show up. Surely he had better things to do, and given how things had ended between them last, he might not want to see her either.

A part of her felt bad about the way she'd reacted. He was trying to protect his uncle, and she tried to imagine if she might, as he'd suggested, do the same, were she in his shoes. But she couldn't. She couldn't imagine shutting down a paper for personal interests. A newspaper wasn't just a source of information, it was a seeker of truth, a light to shine on the best and worst in the world, and a voice for those who otherwise might go unheard.

But he had a right to be suspicious of the *Tribune*, given what had happened...

Kimani blew out a large breath as she tried to focus on the event. She wanted to arrive early to help with setup.

"It's game day, Kimani," she told her reflection in the hallway mirror. She had worn her hair in a double French braid and was dressed in sweats in case she decided to shoot a few hoops herself.

"Good luck with your event," Marissa said. "I wish I didn't have to work so that I could come and help you out."

"I'll be fine, but thanks. I'll see you later," Kimani returned as she left the house with a large gym bag of basketballs draped over her shoulder.

Stepping out—she froze.

But it wasn't Ben this time. Across the street stood a tall, beefy guy she recognized as Vince, Jake's bodyguard, or something like that. He was leaning against a wall, a cigarette sticking from his mouth, casually watching her.

She hadn't thought to include him in the restraining order. Is that how Jake was going to try to intimidate her from now on?

She stared at Vince, whose lips curled in a small smile. She fished out her cellphone and took a picture of him, proof that she needed a restraining order on him, too. He seemed startled and walked away.

It wasn't a damn coincidence that he was there. Despite her best efforts to shake it off, she couldn't help but be unnerved.

Don't let that asshole get the better of you.

Taking a deep breath, she focused on getting herself to East Oakland. She was the first one on site, but a number of volunteers from Gordon's campaign showed up shortly after. They set up tables, the refreshments, and PA system.

"This was such a great idea," Gordon said to Kimani after he had arrived. "I'd love to do more events like this."

"I'm happy to help out," Kimani said.

Her mood had improved since arriving. The weather couldn't be nicer for a mild, sunny autumn day. The turnout was looking good, and kids were already having fun playing ball.

"You plan on playing any ball, Mr. Lee?" she asked playfully.

"I can try," he answered. "It should be good for a laugh or two. But I'll probably leave the ball playing to Ben."

Kimani's breath lodged in her throat. "Is he, uh, coming?"

"I don't know. I mentioned the event to him in passing, and he sounded surprised. I guess I had assumed he knew about it."

She cleared her throat but didn't respond directly to that. Instead, she asked, "All set to kick off the event?"

Microphone in hand, Gordon welcomed everyone and thanked the volunteers and the nonprofit organization.

"And I would especially like to thank Kimani Taylor, who had the idea for this event and who organized it almost single-handedly," he said. He gestured for her to join him. "Let's all give her a great big thank you."

She waved at the crowd as they applauded.

Gordon went on to talk about what the event meant for him and the neighborhood, what he believed needed to be done differently in City Hall to better address the needs of the community, and what values he and his campaign stood for. He kept his remarks brief so that they could get on with the fun parts of the event. Kimani had gotten an old friend from high school to provide some music, and Maybelle showed up with barbecue, beans, and collard greens.

Halfway into the event, they had raised almost five hundred dollars.

"I made a call to the East Bay Neighborhoods Foundation," Gordon said to Kimani, "and the Executive Director there agreed to match the donations we've collected today dollar for dollar."

"That's wonderful!" she exclaimed.

A television reporter interrupted to ask if she could interview Gordon.

"You really ought to be interviewing this extraordinary young woman," he said. "She put it all together."

But Kimani didn't want the limelight. "All I'm going to say is that Gordon inspired me to want to do this."

And before the reporter could say anything, Kimani trotted off. She went to check on the basketballs. Two of them seemed kind of flat, so she pulled out a pump.

"You playing?"

She bobbled the pump and nearly dropped it. Jesus, would she ever get to a point where Ben's appearance didn't totally discombobulated her?

"Maybe later," she answered. Her spirits were high, and she didn't want to be angry at anyone at the moment, especially Ben.

He picked up one of the balls and dribbled it. Finding it had a lackluster bounce, he took the pump. She watched him as he filled the ball with more air. He didn't seem angry with her.

"How about a little one-on-one?" he asked.

She remembered the last time they had played ball together. She had ended up on top of him, and there wasn't much ball playing after that. Actually, they never got back to playing ball at all.

"I've got to make sure the event runs smoothly."

"What's the purpose of this event?"

"Provide Gordon some good PR and raise some money to fix up these courts."

Ben looked over to the reporter still talking to his uncle. "I'd say your first goal has been accomplished. How much have you raised so far?"

"With the matching grant that your uncle secured, we'll probably be close to a thousand."

"You'll want more than a thousand."

"This is a grassroots community event. Most of these folks don't have a ton of spare cash lying around, even for the worthiest causes."

"These courts need more than a little repair work."

She raised her chin. "Have you had a chance to donate yet?"

"I'll play you for it."

Oh no. He had that look. Like he was going to have her for supper.

"What do you mean?"

"You win, I make out a check for five thousand dollars. I win, I get you."

Her throat went dry. "What?"

"I didn't get the full week I paid for. You owe me three days."

Her legs grew weak, but she threw back her shoulders. Even if she was scared on the inside, she wasn't going to show it. "Take that up with Jake. Your deal was with him, not me."

"Too chicken to take me on?"

Her jaw dropped, but she returned his challenge. "You're not going to make a donation out of the goodness of your heart—at an event your own uncle is hosting?"

He grinned. "Why do that when I can play you for it?"

She shook her head. "You're unbelievable."

"What are you afraid of? That you're not going to win the five thousand...or that you're going to be mine for three days?"

Ensnared in his gaze, she had nowhere to hide, nowhere to escape. She was starting to hate rich people. If he didn't have the kind of money he did, he wouldn't be able to throw out crazy-ass propositions. He wouldn't be able to put her in the tough spot of risking her body for a cause that could really use the money. Outside of Ben, she didn't have the connections to raise that sum. How could she deny the neighborhood five thousand dollars? Somewhere in this world, the good guys had to prevail.

But she didn't want to give Ben what he wanted. Maybe it was a childish impulse. Maybe she was being stubborn. Maybe she didn't want to be his little fucktoy. Maybe.

"If you're not going to make a donation because it's the right thing to do," she said, "then you're a pretty damn worthless billionaire."

He raised his brows. There was a look on his face she had never seen before, but she was done talking to him and had turned away from him.

"Actually," she said, turning back. "I'll play you *after* you make a donation. And if I win, you keep the *Tribune* running."

He stared at her. He was going to refuse, but she had to throw it out there. He wasn't the only one who could proposition the other.

"Fine."

She did a double take. He was accepting?

"And if I win," he confirmed, "I get you."

She grabbed the ball out his hands. "You're on, motherfucker."

His brows went up. He stepped toward her, invading her space. It sent her breath scattering.

He lowered his voice. "Talking trash. I'm going to have a lot of fun punishing you for that, pet."

Chapter Twenty

Unable to think up a comeback, Kimani merely dribbled the ball and made her way to the court, as if his words didn't merit a response. She didn't want Ben to see her stumped or the fact that he had rattled her.

Don't pay him any attention.

They watched a three-on-three game finishing up. While she collected herself, she evaluated how she was going to win. Given Ben's height, he could easily block her shots, so she would have to create some space or beat him to the basket. Her shot technique was more solid than his, and that would have to carry the day because defending against him would be hard. He could power his way to the basket.

What had she gotten herself into?

She toyed briefly with the idea of trying to get into his head somehow, but that was perhaps his greatest asset. If she tried to mess with his mind, chances are it would backfire. And if she somehow made him mad, well, he might react as Reggie Miller did in the first game of the 1995 playoff series and lead the Pacers to victory against the Knicks.

"Twenty-one?" Ben asked as the game before them finished.

"Sure," she said, agreeing to the popular version of

street basketball. "How do you play?"

"However you wish."

She went through the rules she knew, and he agreed to the variations.

"Jump ball?" she asked.

He shook his head. "Ladies first."

She took the ball up top and started dribbling. He took a defensive stance before her. She faked right, then driving left, was able to get around him for a layup. In a game of Twenty-one, that meant she got up to three free throws.

"Hey, can we join?" asked a young man from the sidelines.

A crowd was starting to gather.

"No," she answered as she made her free throw.

Nothing but net.

She dribbled the ball in front of her, the familiar feel of leather against her hand coaxing her muscle memory to life. She made her second free throw. Already she was up three to nothing. Eighteen more points to go.

She missed her third and failed to get the rebound. Ben dribbled the ball up top and took a fader over her. The ball bounced off the rim and into the net.

"Lucky motherfucker," she muttered loud enough for him to hear.

He had taken the shot from the three-point line, though in her version of Twenty-one, it counted for two points while all other field goals counted for one. A good three-point shooter had the advantage since a three-point shot was worth twice a two-point shot. Like her, he made two of his free throws, putting him up, four to three.

She beat him to the rebound, dribbled over to half-court, charged toward the basket, pulled back as he continued forward, and drained her own three-pointer. She made all three of her free throws. Now it was eight to four. And she got the ball back. But she missed her jumper.

After taking the ball up top, Ben attacked the basket. She planted herself in the key just as he went into the air for his layup, knocking her to the ground. The ball went in.

"Hey, that ain't cool," one of the spectators said. "Knocking a girl down."

Ben offered her a hand up. "Want me to go more gentle?"

Refusing his hand, she got to her feet. "Hell no."

"That's right, you got girl power," a female encouraged.

Ben made two of his free throws, making him down only one point. They exchanged field goals and free throws, working up a sweat, till she was eventually up nineteen to eighteen. She had the ball for her first throw. If she made the first one, she got a second, and if she made that one, she would get her third. But if she missed, she would drop back down to eleven. She could deliberately miss the free throw, but then Ben might get the rebound and go on a run.

"What's the matter?" Ben asked. "Not confident in

your free throw?"

"Now who's trash-talking?" she returned as she considered what she should do.

He lowered his voice, "When I win, our first night is going to be at The Lair."

She nearly lost her dribble. Best to put an end to the game. She went for the free throw.

And missed.

"Ouch," someone said as the crowd groaned in sympathy.

Ben recovered the ball, took it up top, and backed his way to the basket. He pivoted and drained a jumper over her head.

Shit.

Deciding that two can play head games, she inched in close to him as he prepared to take his free throw shot. "What do you have in mind for The Lair? You want me to go down on you?"

He turned to her and smiled. "Among many things, pet."

His free throw went nothing but net. He made his next free throw and was within one of winning. Her heart clenched. She was going to lose.

But he threw his third shot casually, and it bounced off the rim.

It was almost as if he'd intended to miss. Why would he do that?

But she couldn't dwell on it. She retrieved the ball and took it up top. Most of the crowd was with her and cheered when she made a basket from downtown. She then nailed her three free throws. She could win this. But when her gaze met his, her concentration faltered. Ben stole the ball and dribbled toward the basket.

She caught up to him, but again his height became an advantage. He pulled up, and even though she ended up fouling him on the arm, his shot still went in.

She had lost.

*****

"Come with me," a woman behind the check-in of The Lair told Kimani. It was the redhead who had delivered the invitation that first night.

The night had barely begun, and Kimani was all nerves, like she was the night before the Northern California high school girls' basketball championship. She reminded herself that she had survived four days with Ben. She could survive another three. And part of her was almost *giddy* at the heights he could take her body to. It was getting there, the road to rapture, that frightened her.

"My name's Amanda," said the woman who led her up the stairs to the Upper Balcony. "I'm going to help you get ready."

"I'm sure I'll be fine," Kimani replied.

"I've got specific instructions."

"Really? Like what?"

"Like your bath. I've got the water up already."

"I took a shower—"

"Doesn't matter."

"I don't want my hair to get all wet and frizzy." She touched her hair, which she had sectioned off and pinned into an updo, to make sure it was still in place. The hairstyle was more elegant than the occasion called for, but it had taken relatively little time. Similar to the last time she had come to The Lair, her clothes were casual, consisting of her Converse sneakers, capri-length jeans, and a short-sleeved shirt.

"Don't worry, I won't touch your hair," Amanda said.

Wait, were there places she was going to touch?

Amanda led her to a bathroom, cozy and nicely appointed. The room was lit only with candles and had a deep antique clawfoot tub with a double-slipper silhouette for leaning back at either end.

"So what exactly is the bath for?" Kimani asked, taking in the lavender-scented bath water.

"I'm not sure. I only have instructions on what to do, but I'm guessing it's to put you in the mood." Amanda gave her an encouraging smile.

"What if I don't want a bath?"

Amanda cocked her head to the side in thought. "I'm not sure. You'll have to take it up with your Master."

Kimani stiffened at the last word. He'd probably punish her for not following orders. It was easier taking the bath. No sense in fighting the small stuff.

"Want some help getting settled in?" Amanda asked.

"I can take care of myself. How much time do I get?"

"As long as you need."

How about five hours? But Kimani knew she couldn't hide out in a bath. She should just get on with it. Rip the Band-Aid off as fast as possible.

Amanda set down a glass of water on a table beside the tub. "I'll be back with your outfit."

Kimani frowned, hoping that the outfit did not entail a chastity belt.

After Amanda left, Kimani undressed and slipped into the tub. After a few minutes of soaking in the steaming, scented water, she felt more relaxed. She was also thirsty, so she finished the glass of water on the small table beside the tub.

As she leaned against the tub and closed her eyes, she saw Ben's smoldering gaze. She couldn't tell what he intended. The sex in the Silk Room had been rougher, more punishing than she had ever experienced. Should she expect more of that? It probably depended on how he felt about her...but what exactly did he feel? She wasn't even sure he liked her. She was sure of his anger when he'd told her outside of Gordon's campaign headquarters that she shouldn't bother making up for what she had done. And she would never forget the look of betrayal after finding out about the *Tribune* article on his uncle.

After all that, he still wanted her. Maybe he just wanted to prove a point. Maybe he did want his money's worth. Maybe he wanted to punish her.

Despite the heat of the bath embracing her body, she shivered. She would sooner run the baseline or do half an hour of burpees.

What are you, crazy? The sex is mind-blowing.

But burpees were so much safer.

She knew what to expect with burpees. What if Ben didn't let her come? What if it was going to be pain without the pleasure?

When has he not let you come?

Memories of her time with Ben flashed through her mind: squirming in his lap as he finger-fucked her on the patio of Jake's lakeside cabin; making her squirt for the first time; tied to the chair on Jake's boat with her bikini bottom stuffed into her mouth; exhausted and exhilarated after he had wrung ten orgasms in a row out of her; coming undone in his arms as the shower jets blasted her; and having her ass penetrated with his hardness.

Even though she sat in water, she could feel a different sort of wetness develop. Would her arousal be helpful or not tonight?

"How is the bath?" Amanda asked upon returning. She handed Kimani another glass of water. "Your Master would like you to stay hydrated."

Kimani balked at the word again and wondered if she would ever get used to it. She took the towel Amanda held out to her and dried herself, including the area between her legs.

"Here's your bra and panties," Amanda said, casually holding a cup-less shelf bra of red satin and black lace trim, and a matching crotch-less thong.

At least it wasn't a chastity belt, Kimani thought ruefully to herself as her cheeks burned. She slid on the lingerie.

"And here are your stockings and shoes."

Kimani pulled on the thigh-high nylons with elasticized lace tops, then stared at the black platform sandals with ridiculously high heels.

"Those are not my kind of shoes."

"They were all I was given. I think they're amazingly hot. You'll look great in them."

Amanda helped her into the shoes. ""You'll be in the Dungeon. I'll show you where it is."

The Dungeon. That did not sound promising.

"Can I at least throw a robe or some clothes on top?"

"Your Master didn't say you could."

"But he probably didn't say I couldn't, either."

"True. Well, it's up to you if you want to take that chance."

Kimani decided it was probably best not to risk it.

"Your Master did allow for a mask if you wanted some anonymity."

From a dresser that had three mannequin heads with wigs and masks, she plucked off a black satin mask.

"You look super sexy," Amanda said after Kimani had affixed the mask to her face.

And ready for the slaughter, Kimani thought to herself.

She followed Amanda down another set of stairs and through a room not unlike the one on the main floor of The Lair. In one corner, a woman of Indian descent was flogging her partner. On the sofa in the middle of the room, a transsexual was thrusting her hips into the man before her. Though neither couple paid too much attention to Amanda and Kimani, Kimani still felt as if she was being paraded through the room.

Amanda took her through a set of curtains into a room that appeared the opposite of the Silk Room. Instead of silk wallpaper, the walls of the Dungeon appeared to be the original concrete of the converted warehouse. Like Ben's playroom, there was a St. Andrew's cross and a wrought-iron bed with a mattress. There was also a rack and pillory.

"Have fun," said Amanda before she left

Kimani swallowed.

Game on.

Chapter Twenty-One

Bloody amazing.

When Ben had picked out the lingerie, he knew they were going to look sexy on Kimani, but when he walked into the Dungeon, what he saw exceeded all expectation. The lingerie was the best damn purchase he had ever made. He liked the look of black lace on her dark skin, and her breasts, pushed up by the bra, looked fucking amazing. Her areolas made his mouth water.

He had chosen to dress the part as well, sporting leather pants and a tight-fitting black tee. Walking over to her, he made an obvious sweep of her from head to toe with his stare. She shivered beneath his devouring gaze.

All this beauty was his. She was all his.

Kimani didn't know it, but she had walked into a setup with his challenge. He had known that she'd want to win the donation and possibly avoid being his for three days. That was a lot riding on her shoulders. She was the kind of person to put a lot of pressure on herself, and that had affected her game. He didn't mentioned that, win or lose, he was going to make the donation.

"Whoever invented five-inch heels was a real misogynist," she declared.

"So what does it say about women that you're willing to wear them?"

"I don't wear shoes like these."

"Not even for fun?"

"Maybe once. At a Halloween party. So, I guess for fun. But it's complicated. As a woman, you wonder if wearing shoes like these means you're pandering to men, letting them define what's sexy, and objectifying yourself. On the other hand, if you want to be strong and sexy, and you like wearing heels like these, you get slut-shamed. It's a no-win situation."

Was she stalling or talking because she was nervous? If he weren't so eager to ravish her, he would indulge the discussion, but the Dungeon wasn't a place for intellectual musings. The Dungeon was for sex. Wicked, kinky sex.

He looked at the half-empty glass of water she held. "Finish your water."

While she drank, he retrieved a cord of rope.

She had finished the water, leaving a few ice cubes at the bottom. Fishing one out with his finger, he circled it around her areola. The cold made her gasp. He moved the ice closer to her nipple. She gasped louder, squeaking when the ice passed over the tip. The bud hardened nicely. He dropped what was left of the ice into the glass, which he took from her and set aside. Rope in hand, he began to bind her wrists.

"There are only two simple rules to follow," he told her. "One, addressing properly every time you speak. Try it."

She glared. "Yes, Sir."

"Second, if you want to come, you have to beg for it. Got that?"

"Yes, Sir."

"Good pet."

She bristled.

Having finished tying her wrists, he threw the excess rope over a wooden beam overhead. The beam was there for suspension bondage, which he hoped to incorporate into tonight's scene. Stepping back, he appraised how hot she looked. He walked behind her to view her backside. Her heels caused her arse to stick out, and he couldn't resist palming her full buttocks, digging his fingers into the ample flesh.

Returning to stand in front of her, he played with her breasts, gently kneading, then roughly groping. He roused the other nipple to match the hardness of the first, tugging it, pinching it, twisting it. She grunted and squeaked while squirming. He slapped a breast when she squirmed too much. She stilled her movement and submitted to his manhandling.

"That's better," he said before sharply slapping her breasts a few more times.

Her brows knit in anger. She was probably wondering why he was slapping her when she was doing exactly what he wanted.

He fisted his hand into her hair and, yanking her head back, explained to her, "You see, pet, I get to do whatever the fuck I want to do to you. In general, it's always wiser to obey your Master. Unless you want to be punished for disobedience, and that's a lot more fun for me than it is for you, given you're not a hardcore masochist. Do you remember your safety word?"

"Mercy."

"Good. You might need it tonight."

He wrapped an arm around her waist and pulled her to him so that she could feel his hard-on. Releasing her head, he reached between her thighs and found her damp. The slick moisture was not the water from the bath.

"You always get wet for me, don't you?"

Fuck you, her eyes said.

He gave her a light slap across the cheek. "Don't you?"

Yes, Sir," she mumbled.

Fitting his fingers through the opening in her panties, he caressed her till her breath grew erratic and her lashes started to flutter. When he withdrew his fingers, she whimpered. He rubbed the moisture his fingers had collected onto a nipple before he licked and sucked the nectar of her arousal off her breast.

Next, he retrieved a suitcase containing his violet wand kit that retailed for over a thousand dollars. Setting it on a small table near her, he took out the wand, fixed the glass rod electrode to it, and plugged it into the outlet. Her eyes had widened and her breath shortened.

"Is that going to hurt?" she asked, staring skeptically at the wand.

"A lot of things are going to hurt tonight, pet," he

answered as he looked her over to make sure she wasn't wearing any jewelry that might unexpectedly draw a charge.

She glanced sharply at him. He could practically see her adrenaline spike.

"All the same, you're going to want it...and more," he assured her, turning the wand on low and testing it against his own skin.

He then brushed the wand over her nylons, which provided a nice gap for the charge to be felt. She gasped, mostly from surprise, but since he was applying the broad side of the rod, the charge was spread out and should have felt like champagne bubbles fizzing against her skin.

"Does my pet like that?"

"I, um, I guess," she admitted, "so far."

He smiled. She knew it wasn't going to remain this tame. He moved the wand over her hip, across the buttocks, up the back, and over a shoulder. She braced herself when the wand came near her breasts, gasping loudly when the underwire in her bra drew the charge.

After several minutes of warming her up, he switched out the rod for the body contact cable. He fixed one end to the wand and placed the other end inside his pants. Now his body became the conductor of electricity.

He grabbed her breast. The touch of flesh on flesh grounded out the charge, but when he slowly withdrew his hand, he created the gap needed for the spark. When he hovered his hand over her nipple, she started to whimper.

He went to stand behind her, roaming his hand above the swell of her buttocks, which he grasped, kneaded, and slapped.

"God, your arse is bloody gorgeous," he murmured, smacking it harder. "Does it want to be properly fucked tonight?"

"Maybe," she replied. "How about you make that childcare center Dawson Chang wants happen, and I'll let you into my arse."

Her response stunned him. She turned around and looked at him as if to say, "Two can play at this game."

"You working for Dawson Chang now?" he asked. He wasn't particularly happy with the head of the Asian Pacific Community Alliance, who was still holding out on his endorsement in the mayoral race to gain concessions like the one Kimani had just stated.

"No, but it's the right thing to do," she said. "You get to develop your property, and the community gets an important need met."

"Economic development is a public benefit."

"In a trickle down way. Build a childcare center and that's something of value with an immediate impact."

He stared at her arse. There was no way he was leaving tonight without having a piece of that.

"I won't guarantee it'll be on the waterfront property," he said, "but I'll make something happen off-site."

Shit. He couldn't believe he had agreed to that. He hadn't wanted to give in to Dawson's tactics. But he was impressed by Kimani's play and didn't want her to go away empty-handed, especially since he had taken away her job.

He grabbed her around the waist and pulled her arse into his crotch, grinding his erection into her. He yanked her head back by her hair.

"Since we're negotiating," he said, "how about I double my donation for those basketball courts if you can refrain from using your safety word."

Releasing her hair, he reached over for the wand to turn up the setting. He held his hand near her hip. She yelped at the stronger charge. He reached between her legs. She tried to move away from his hand, backing her arse farther into him in the process, but she ultimately had nowhere to go.

"Oh, Jeeeesus," she murmured as his fingers electrified her pussy.

He alternated between touching her and sparking her body. He rubbed her clit, getting it to swell, then pulled back enough for her to feel the charge. Soon, it seemed she couldn't decide if she wanted his hand between her legs or not. Either way, she got wetter.

"Spread 'em wider," he said, pulling her thighs apart.

He sat on the floor between her legs and inhaled her scent. Blood pounded in his head. Grabbing her by the thighs, he tongued her clit. She yelped and made sounds halfway between a laugh and a cry. He held her in place as he used his tongue as an electrode. When he granted her a reprieve by touching his tongue to her, she ground herself into him, not wanting him to create the gap for sparks to fly, wanting to stay with pleasure over pain. He brought her to the edge, to where she was groaning and her eyes were rolled toward the back of her head.

Would she remember to ask permission?

He continued applying his tongue to her engorged clit, varying the licking and sucking, sliding the tip over her urethra and teasing her slit till her legs quivered. He didn't need to go faster or harder. He knew the spot that would send her over the edge, and when he decided to give her the climax she sought, he just had to attend it steadily.

Her body shook, first from the orgasm, then from the charge that sparked when he released her. She cried out when he shocked her again.

She shuddered. "Oh...my...God."

He rose to his feet and observed her flushed cheeks and half-lidded eyes. She looked beautiful.

"Good news is you didn't use your safety word," he said as he removed the cable. "Bad news is you forgot to ask permission."

Chapter Twenty-Two

uck.

Life was so unfair, Kimani thought to herself.

"What's the matter?" Ben asked, noticing the look on her face.

"You want to know the truth?" she asked.

"I've told you before that my problem is with lies. I don't have a problem with the truth."

"Let's see...you're the asshole who shut down the *Tribune* and took away my job, yet I'm the one getting punished here?"

He brushed his thumb over her lower lip. "Poor baby. Life's unfair, isn't it?"

She yanked at her bound wrists as if she wanted her hands free to scratch his face. Why had she ever agreed to the one-on-one with this guy? How could she have been so stupid? She didn't want to give him access to her ass anymore. Never mind that he just performed the best damn cunnilingus she had ever had. She felt her initial anger at discovering he was behind the *Tribune's* closure all over again.

But a childcare center...that was huge. She hadn't thought he would agree to it. She remembered that Ben had not been happy with Dawson's demands, and thought a childcare center made no economic sense for the property his family was developing. But finding a location that made financial sense for the Lee Family Corporation that also worked for the community would not be easy.

She knew he liked her ass, but enough to agree to build a childcare center? When the city might have let the development get away with a contribution to the city's affordable housing pool, a public plaza, or something less challenging? She wasn't sure *she* liked her own ass enough to make such a concession.

Still, this was fifty shades of messed up...wasn't it? Only the character in that story wasn't nearly as big a jerk as the guy standing in front of her.

Ben looked at her with emotions she couldn't read.

"You hate me, don't you?" he inquired.

"Why, does that turn you on?" she retorted.

He contemplated. "Sure. The thought that you might hate me, yet you still come for me, screaming and shaking...yeah, that turns me on."

Ugh. Why was there no winning with this guy? He always had the upper hand somehow.

Was there a way to end this game? Should she forfeit so that she could go back to the relative safety of her home? Maybe she'd rather encounter the intruder again.

No, that would be foolish. As much as he aggravated her, she trusted that he wouldn't allow her to come to any real harm. With Ben, she ultimately felt safe.

He cupped her jaw and drew her to him. "Hate me as much you want. I'm the big bad foreign developer who suppresses freedom of the press. But you'll still come for me over and over again, pet."

She stared into the depths of his eyes, unable to deny the truth of what he said. She wanted to reply that the body had a mind of its own, which was only partially or sometimes true. If someone other than Ben did what he did to her, she wouldn't be aroused. She would be the victim of assault.

So the truth was, she didn't hate Ben. At least not a hundred percent. But she wasn't going to admit that to him.

Only he knew it already. And he was going to use that to his advantage.

"What's the most you've ever come for me in one night?" Ben mused aloud. "Ten? We'll top that tonight."

Her legs went weak, and not just because her high heels were making her sore.

He dropped her jaw and replaced the cord of his electrical wand with a ball-tip probe.

"And you'll want to ask permission before you come each time, or it's going to be long night," he warned before zapping her.

She screamed. He hadn't increased the setting, but the new electrode managed to concentrate the charge, making it a lot more intense. He pointed it at her breast.

"Motherfucker!" she exclaimed, backing her body away from him.

He zapped her from behind, stinging her buttock,

making her body strain the other direction. He came at her from all sides, and because she was strung up, she couldn't escape. She thought about using the safety word.

"You better...be telling...the truth," she said between difficult breath, "about that donation."

"I promise," he said before zapping her inner thigh.

"Oh, God! I hate you."

He waved the wand toward her nipple. "I could be a real motherfucking asshole and fix some metal clamps to your nipples. Then charge them up with the wand."

"No! I mean, please don't...sir."

He seemed pleased. "What do you suggest I do instead?"

"You want my ass, don't you?"

A muscle along his jaw rippled. "More than anything, pet. But I'm saving the best for last."

"Then how about a blow job?" She licked her bottom lip for effect. Anything to avoid getting her nipples electrocuted. "You liked the head I gave before."

"I did. Does my pet want my cock in her mouth?"

She nodded and panted like a dog, even though the petplay they had done at Jake's cabin wasn't one of her favorite moments.

He chuckled and put away the wand.

"All right, pet," he said after he had untied her arms from the beam. He unzipped his pants and drew out a very stiff cock. "It's all yours."

Though the concrete floor wasn't going to be comfortable on her knees, she was glad to be off her feet. She settled before him and, grabbing his shaft, she licked the tip. With her tongue, she swept away the glisten of pre-cum, then lapped at the underside of the flare, before fitting her mouth over the top. He moaned as she sank down his cock.

Up and down she went, sucking and laving her tongue along his length. He fisted his hand through her hair, gently guiding her lower. She relaxed her throat to take more of him. Somehow she managed not to choke. From before, she had learned her lesson not to expend her energy too fast in an attempt to get him to come quickly. Then, she hadn't known about his crazy Taoist practice of orgasming without ejaculating.

Only when his groans grew louder and more shallow did she increase her vigor.

With a curse, he thrust his hips. She gagged when his cock hit the back of her throat at an unexpected angle, but she recovered. She cradled his balls and stretched her fingers to rub his perineum. He cursed just before he came, pulling her off him before stumbling back. His eyes were closed in concentration, and she imagined he might have been fighting back the ejaculation. After a moment of deep breathing, he shook his head and opened his eyes.

"Well done, pet."

She stared with amazement at his cock, still rock hard. Even though it had been tough to take at times, she wanted that cock inside her. Remembering how ruthlessly he had drilled into her the last time, she shivered. But, still, she wanted him.

Grabbing the rope around her wrists, he pulled her up, caught the back of her head, and smothered his mouth over hers. In an instant, she found herself drowning. She kissed him back to keep from being too brutalized by the kiss. Sometimes the best defense was a good offense. And she didn't like that she often found herself forced into a passive role with him. Granted, the submission freed her to enjoy the moment and experience the most exhilarating orgasms, but sometimes she wanted to be more than his plaything to be used, teased and tormented however he liked.

Scooping her up into his arms, he walked over to the bed. Their lips remained locked as she knelt upon the mattress. He tasted good, he smelled good, a heady mix of raw lust, masculinity, and controlled power.

She gripped his shirt and pulled him closer, matching every thrust of his tongue with her own. She slid her hands beneath his shirt and caressed his abdominal muscles, moving up to his pectorals. He peeled off his shirt, and she devoured his upper body with her stare before diving for a nipple. She licked, tongued, and sucked. He allowed her to assault the hardened bud, then pinched one of her nipples to indicate she should stop.

She hoped that she hadn't gone too far. He could make her pay all too easily.

Chapter Twenty-Three

Kimani looked at him tentatively. Maybe she thought he was going to punish her. Ben let her think that for now. In the right doses, fear could serve to enhance the senses.

Climbing onto the bed, he pulled her down and tied the rope to the bars of the headboard.

"Still taking my offer not to use your safety word?" he asked as he gently massaged her breast. "Ten thousand dollars will buy brand-new courts and then some."

"What do you have in mind?" she replied. "I don't want my nipples getting burned with electricity."

"We'll work up to that."

She frowned, not liking his joke.

He reached over to the bedside table where he had placed a ball gag. "This'll help if you're worried you might need the safety word."

She stared at the gag, then at him, probably wondering whether or not to trust him. He hadn't made it easy. She knew he was capable of wicked things, so she would have to trust that he would take her to her limits but not past them. So far in their play, he had done just that, but the past wasn't a perfect predictor of the future.

Or maybe she was willing to sacrifice her body for

a neighborhood in need, willing to be a martyr. That would make him feel like an even bigger asshole. But he'd make it up to her.

"It's up to you," he said. "You could walk out of here with a childcare center and new basketball courts."

It sounded preposterous. He had never negotiated sex before, but with Kimani, he found himself doing things he never expected to.

She pursed her lips. "I've got to trust that you're going to come through."

"You do," he said tenderly, then changed his tone, not wanting to sound too soft. "You're actually getting quite the deal, pet. I've got other ways of getting you to do what I want."

She glared at him. "Fine. Give me the damn gag."

Maybe she felt she didn't have much of a choice in the matter, but the possibility that she did trust him meant a lot. He slid the ball between her lips and secured the leather strap about her head. He sat back. No mouth could look hotter.

He rubbed various parts of her and planted kisses upon her breasts, belly, and thighs. With the gag in her mouth, taking away her primary form of communication, her eyes appeared even larger. They watched his every move.

After worshipping the landscape of her body, he lay beside her and caressed her between the legs. She was very, very wet. He rolled his thumb over her clit and noticed how her breath changed. After toying with her clit, he slid his digits over her slit, teasing her but not entering until it seemed she wriggled her hips in invitation. He sank a digit into her wet heat, then two. Curling his fingers, he felt the roof of her pussy. She moaned as he strummed the raised area. He pushed down on her pubic bone, collapsing the vagina about his fingers. She tried to talk through the gag in her mouth.

He knew what she was asking. "You're wondering how you're going to ask permission to come when you've got a gag in your mouth."

She nodded.

"That is a problem," he acknowledged.

She gave him a stare that suggested she wanted to see him six feet under right now.

"Do your best," he said. "You can try begging with your eyes."

He heard her swallow, which wasn't easy with the ball gag stretching her mouth. At first she reacted like a sulking child, not wanting to engage, trying her best to resist his ministrations. But either she couldn't resist what his fingers were doing, or she realized that holding out on coming was only delaying the inevitable, because she wasn't going anywhere till he had gotten ten-plus orgasms out of her. Now when she writhed, it was because she was approaching her climax. He loved the way her brows knit, her nostrils flared, and her body trembled as the rapture neared its peak.

"Mmm uh kuh, er?" she asked, which translated as,

"May I come, Sir?"

"Come, and don't hold it in," he reminded her, fucking her vigorously with his fingers before pulling them out. A stream of wetness followed. He plunged his fingers back in, jerked his hand, and yanked them back out to release another stream.

She screamed into the gag and shivered atop the bed. He gently caressed her as she tried to draw large breaths through her nose, which was not as efficient as her mouth with taking in air. He watched her contract between the legs and stroked himself with his free hand.

Deciding he wanted to come again as well—it would help him last longer when he decided to fuck her with his cock later, he straddled her across the chest. He reached beneath her to unhook her bra before pushing it above her breasts. He squeezed the orbs together about his erection and began to thrust. God, how he loved using every part of her body. The friction of her silken skin against him soon had him ascending his own climax.

He would leave his mark on her, brand her as his. No one else was going to access an inch of her without his permission.

The thought drove him over the edge. He grabbed his cock and jerked himself off, shooting his cum over her breasts and collarbone. A few drops made it to her neck and chin. She looked fucking beautiful with his white semen glistening off her dark skin. He pulled the ball gag down and aimed his shaft at her mouth. She took him in and cleaned him off.

"Good pet," he praised, then replaced the ball gig.

After zipping his pants, he retrieved a Hitachi. Turning it on, he held it to her clit. Within minutes, she was moaning anew. Cradling the wand in the V of his middle and forefinger, he inserted his middle and ring finger into her sodden slit.

"Uhhhh..." she moaned into the gag.

Holding the vibrator to her while he fucked her with his fingers, he had her close to coming for the third time tonight. He glanced at her face. She stared at him with wide, intense eyes.

May I come? they asked.

"You may," he assented.

She threw her head back and fell into spasms. He held the Hitachi in place till she tried to scramble away from it. He turned it off and watched her as she panted. She mumbled something, but he couldn't tell what she intended to say, if anything. He allowed her a respite as he caressed her body with his free hand, grabbing a breast, slapping it to keep her alert.

"You're not fading on me, are you?" he asked. "We're not even halfway through."

He rubbed the wand over her vulva, then sank two fingers back into her pussy. This time, he felt for the floor of her vagina, strumming and bouncing his fingers off her cervix. She grunted when he grabbed her pubic bone, then groaned. He vibrated his hand, twisted his fingers, alternating between her G-spot and the cervix. She babbled something into her gag.

Withdrawing his fingers, he flipped her onto her stomach and pulled her onto her elbows and knees, doggy style. He switched the Hitachi back on, cradled it in his hand once more, and sank his thumb into her. He sawed the shorter but thicker digit in and out.

"Mmm uh kuh, er?"

"What's the magic word?" he asked.

"Pwheee."

"Good pet. You may come."

With his thumb, he pressed her G-spot down into the vibrator. Within a minute, she was undone, screaming, shaking, and squirting. He caressed her rump till her body had calmed and all the shivers had dissipated. As he beheld her perfectly rounded ass, he wondered that he could save the best for last.

He unzipped his pants and pulled out his erection. He stroked it to full hardness, then took out a condom from his pocket. After putting it on, he adjusted her panties to make sure he had uninterrupted entry into her pussy. He sank into her. And she felt just as marvelous as the last time. He could easily feel her heat through the condom. He would never tire of being inside her.

Slowly, he moved his hips, testing how deep he could bury his cock. Bracing himself on one arm, he reached around to play with her clit till she was fully aroused again. Then he straightened, grabbed her hips, and began a steady thrusting, occasionally throwing in a hard pounding to keep her guessing. He loved the sound of his pelvis smacking into her arse. He settled on the angle that elicited the best reaction from her.

As she became worked up, he slowed. She started pushing her arse at him, impaling herself on his cock. He allowed her to fuck him till he sensed her tiring. Holding her in place, he took over. Her grunts grew in excitement, pleading and demanding to fall apart in ecstasy. He drove her there before seeking his own end, drilling and shoving his hips into her till euphoria flooded his body like sunshine invading a dark space.

They collapsed onto the bed, both breathing hard, both perspiring. He untied the rope from the bed and pulled her into him. His cum had started to dry on her, and saliva had slid past the ball gag. He undid the gag...because she actually might need her safety word for what came next.

*****

After having her drink some water, Ben removed her bra and soaking panties. He left her damp nylons on and strung her up to the beam again. Next, he retrieved a remote-controlled vibrating egg, an item she was familiar with. He slipped it into her, turned it on to low, and watched her close her eyes, her body soaking up the vibration as much as possible. The low setting would keep her arousal at a nice simmer. He wrapped a silk blindfold over her eyes before fetching his single-tailed whip. He had only used floggers with wider falls with her before.

"What's your safety word?" he asked.

"Am I going to need it?"

"I don't know. I assume you've never experienced a bullwhip."

"Uh, no," she said with a tremor.

"This is going to deliver a sharper sting than the floggers I've used on you before. You ready?"

She pressed her lips together, then answered, "Yes, Sir."

Though The Lair was good about cleaning its facilities, he surveyed the floor to make sure there was nothing that the whip could accidentally pick up. Her hair was out of the way, allowing him to strike her upper back. Since he hadn't used this particular whip of his in a while, he practiced slicing the air, listening for when the crack occurred. She jumped every time.

Standing in front of her, he couldn't see apprehension in her eyes, but he could sense it coming off her body. "Use your safety word if you need it."

"I won't. You're going to owe me brand-new basketball courts."

Emotion swelled in his chest. He crushed his mouth to hers, feeling as if his heart might burst if he couldn't expel some of his feelings through her while at the same time breathing her in, melding her to him.

But he wanted her to get the basketball courts, so he stepped back behind her. He aimed for where she had more muscle and flesh, the upper back and buttocks.

The first whip made her cry out. Blindfolded, she couldn't know when or where he would strike. He started with predictability, swinging the whip at a steady rhythm from left to right on a single plane parallel to the floor, striking her upper back. Then he began to vary the angle and the target. At the same time, he increased the setting on the egg. He walked around her so that he could land the whip on her breasts and her belly. He kept his strokes on the lighter side. Even so, her body might be sensitive to putting on clothes later. He once had a sub who didn't want to wear clothes for two days after.

He circled back behind her. "Spread your legs."

She did as told, then screamed when the whip landed on her pussy. He waited to see if she needed her safety word. She didn't. He rewarded her by increasing the vibrations of the egg. When she got more advanced, he could take two whips to her.

When. It was an appealing thought—going beyond their three days, instructing her on how to become a better submissive, showcasing all that he could do with her.

"Ohhh...may I come, Sir?" she groaned.

"Come."

He turned the setting of the egg to its highest.

"Oh, God!" she cried out.

She writhed and squirmed, not unlike a fish flaying at the end of a hook. Her legs gave way, and she would have crumpled to the floor if she wasn't tied to the beam.

He curled the whip. Next up: suction and suspension.

Chapter Twenty-Four

We're more than halfway there. Hopefully.

As with the last time Ben had made her endure double-digit orgasms in a single night, Kimani had wondered if she could last that long, but her body remained aroused and ready. The single tail had stung, but it hadn't been as bad as she had thought, except when he pussy-whipped her. The motherfucker.

But she had never felt more alive. And the orgasms had been *intense*. During the whipping, as her climax washed over her, she felt as if she had been lifted to a different plane of existence.

Now, suspended in air, her body cradled in rope, she was curious for what would come next. Her arms were tied behind her this time, and her thighs were forced apart, but the bondage was relatively comfortable. From the images she had seen in his playroom, she knew there were much harder positions he could have bound her in. He was taking into account that she was a beginner.

"Are you familiar with cupping?" he asked, holding a wooden box containing a hand pump and several glass cups of varying sizes.

She shook her head.

"It's an ancient Chinese therapy used to reduce

pain and promote relaxation. But we're going to use it to increase sensitivity."

After setting down the small chest, he eyed her pussy and selected a medium-sized cup. He applied a lubricant to the rim, then placed the cup over her vulva. He applied the pump, drawing her clit and labia into the glass. She stared aghast at how her flesh flushed from the suction. He pumped again.

"How is it?" he inquired.

"Uh...okay," she replied. The constant tugging on her most intimate body parts felt unnatural but not painful.

He applied the pump once more. Now her flesh filled almost the entire cup. He disengaged the pump and selected a small glass tube from his kit. After applying lubricant to the rim, he fit the tube over her nipple.

Jesus.

He applied the pump, sucking the bud into the tube. He repeated the process on the other nipple.

This is crazy, she thought as she looked over her body, two glass rods protruding from her beasts and a glass dome filled with her vulva. She watched him slip a cock ring on the Hitachi, which he turned on and applied to the cup between her legs.

"Feel nice?" he asked.

She nodded.

"How did you like the single tail?"

"How would you like getting your cock whipped?" she returned.

"On its own, it's not something I'd seek out. But mixed with pleasure, it's a different story."

"No pain, no gain?"

"Exactly. So, would you do it again?"

"Maybe."

A corner of his lips curled in a small smile. "Anytime you want a whipping, don't hesitate to ask."

"Can I get another donation? I'm sure there's a lot that could use fixing up in that part of East Oakland."

"You're getting greedy, pet," he said, but he seemed amused. "Before long you'll have me setting up a nonprofit organization to fund all kinds of community projects."

She smiled. "That's a great idea!"

He passed the wand over the top of the cup. "You'd have to be my pet for a lot longer than three days."

His gaze met hers. Would he want her for more than three days? Would she want to be his?

Focus on the present, Kimani. You haven't even survived the first day with him yet.

Turning off the Hitachi, he set it aside. He broke the seal on the cup.

"Your pussy looks amazing," he said, as he rubbed two fingers along the sides of the reddened flesh. "Nice and swollen."

He passed a finger over her clit, and she shuddered violently.

Holy...

He shed his pants, put on another condom, and rubbed his cock over her engorged folds and clit. She

228

gasped.

"Sensitive?"

"Very."

He slapped his cock repeatedly against her clit. She groaned and squirmed in her bonds. He masturbated her with his cock, and it didn't take long before the sensations burst into rapture. Her body convulsed and swung in the ropes. He stilled her, then adjusted the ropes so that she was suspended on her side. She felt his cock at her entry.

"Ohmygawd," she moaned when only his tip pushed through.

"Damn," he breathed. "Your pussy's tighter than most arseholes."

She was swollen on the inside, too, so his cock felt huge. She wailed when his erection went deeper.

"Breathe," he reminded her.

I can't.

She closed her eyes and tried to relax. She had never before felt this full. When she thought she had a handle on being stuffed, he sank more of himself into her. He thumbed her clit, lighting up the region between her legs.

"Please, Sir, may I come?" she asked. It was early, but she wasn't sure she would remember to ask when he got going.

He chuckled. "You're getting better and better, pet, though you did miss one."

"Besides that first time?"

"On your fifth orgasm."

"Which one was that?"

"You were getting a nice fucking doggy style."

"That was when I had that gag on."

"You were still supposed to ask."

She looked away so he wouldn't see her roll her eyes. Shit.

"So what's the punishment?" she ventured, then wondered if it was better not to ask.

He withdrew, walked over to his table of wickedness, and returned with a pair of butterfly clamps joined by a small link chain.

Shit. Shit. Shit.

Breaking the seal of the glass tubes, he popped them off. The nipple and surrounding area had become puffy and darker in hue. He circled his fingers around her nipple. She whimpered. Her nipples tended to be sensitive. Now they were going to be off-the-charts sensitive. She braced herself when he lowered his head and flicked his tongue over a hardened bud.

"Jesus!" she cried out, trying somehow to scramble away.

"Be a good pet," he ordered, grabbing her breast.

He licked her again, sending a bolt through her nipple to her pussy, where a craving grew anew. He then placed his entire mouth over the area of her nipple and sucked. The force of his mouth was far greater than the cups. She practically sobbed.

When he came off, he asked, "Don't you want to thank me for punishing you, so that you can become a better submissive?"

Hell no. But he knew that, knew that she wanted to curse him, and that was why he asked the question.

"Thank you, Sir," she replied through gritted teeth.

He fixed one of the clamps near the outer diameter of her areola. Seeing that she seemed okay with the placement, he moved it closer to her nipple.

"Ohhhh..." she groaned.

And closer.

"Oh, fuck," she swore.

He took his hand off the clamp, letting gravity tug at the clamp and consequently her nipple. He applied the other clamp.

New basketball courts, she reminded herself. New basketball courts. New basketball...

He went back to stand at her other end and slapped his cock against her still swollen pussy. The delicious sensation there partially offset the pain on her nipples. He pushed himself into her, filling her. He felt so large, so hard. But once she adjusted to the penetration, his movements, which he kept slow and gentle, began to draw pleasure. The angle was different, his cock touching her in places that hadn't received as much attention before. It felt good. *He* felt good.

He always felt good.

He fondled her clit again, stoking her arousal. He thrust a little harder, a little deeper. The motion made the clamps swing, pulling more painfully on her nipples, but the yearning in her pussy had gone past the point of no return. She needed and wanted release.

It didn't matter how hard he shoved, she'd take it all if only he could get her to that pinnacle of pleasure and send her over.

He grabbed her leg to leverage himself deeper, harder, faster.

"Fuck...oh, fuck," she babbled. "*Fuuuuck*."

She exploded. Her body couldn't contain the burst of tension so scintillating, euphoric, and powerful. It felt as if her body were a live wire, the voltage going through it blowing her mind and rendering her helpless, a mess of spasms and supreme carnal bliss.

Chapter Twenty-Five

While her pussy was still swollen, he sought her ninth orgasm. Laying Kimani on the bed, Ben spooned her. He lifted her top leg to give him easier access to her pussy. He could see she was starting to tire, but she moaned when he sank his cock between her swollen folds. He cupped her breast and played with her still-sensitive nipple. She had looked fucking amazing in sideways suspension, her breasts jiggling to and fro, the clamps swinging from them, her hair coming undone.

He slid his hand between her thighs and fondled her there, his fingers brushing against his own shaft as he pistoned in and out of her. Her orgasm took a little longer to build this time, and she would have forgotten to ask for permission if he hadn't prompted her. Her body clenched on his cock as she erupted. He slammed his hips into her, smacking his pelvis against her arse to achieve his own orgasm.

"You're almost there, pet," he said, brushing his lips over her ear after they had rested for several minutes. He savored the feel of holding her in his arms, her damp body still hot against him.

"I don't know if I can make it," she sighed.

"You won't with that mindset. You want that childcare center, don't you?"

"Right."

"It's the fourth quarter. Final minutes. Starters have been in most of the game, but the coach is counting on you."

She chuckled. "Yeah, but I think I'd rather take on Tennessee or Connecticut."

He flipped her onto her back and smiled. "Can the Huskies do *this*?"

He rolled his thumb over her clitoris and inserted his fingers into her snatch and hit the G-spot. She moaned and fluttered her lashes rapidly.

"Though the thought of you taking on five women," he pondered aloud. "I might defer to that, too."

Kimani getting gang-banged in hot lesbian action would be hard to beat.

"How 'bout it?" he asked as he fondled her and watched as she caressed herself from her belly to her breasts.

"How 'bout what?" she asked dreamily.

"There are members here who would probably jump your bones in a heartbeat."

She stared at him, wondering if he was serious.

"I can make it happen."

"I'm sure you'd like to," she said. "What is it about girl on girl for guys?"

He drew her wetness to the puckered hole below. A lot of her moisture had already dripped there, but it would need more lubrication.

"Does guy-on-guy action not turn you on?"

"It's okay. Probably depends on my mood. But I doubt it has the same effect girl on girl has for you."

He coated his pinky finger with her juices and slowly inserted it into her anus. She drew in a sharp breath, then relaxed at the intrusion.

"What would you offer for me to make out with another woman?"

He stared at her, stunned. It was his turn to wonder if she was serious. Part of him didn't want to share her, even with another woman, but he'd be a bloody moron to pass up such an erotic opportunity.

"A lot," he admitted.

He applied a thumb to her clit, two digits in her slit, and one in her arsehole.

"Yeah? How much?" she managed to ask between moans.

"Don't go down that road unless you're serious."

She pursed her lips. "Well, I wouldn't go crazy and do more than one woman at a time."

He envisioned Kimani kissing another woman, their soft, supple lips joining over and over. Then he imagined them caressing each other, feeling each other up, masturbating each other. His hard-on was ready to burst.

Sitting up, he pulled off the condom and lubed his cock. Time to pony up a childcare center.

He spread her legs wide, then aimed himself at her nether hole. She gave a loud groan when he sank the bulb of his cock into her tightness.

She felt every bit as glorious as he'd expected. He

could feel the walls of her anus press against him, instinctively trying to push out the intruder, but he held his cock in place as he used his other hand to fondle her clit. When she was further aroused, he sank more of his cock into her.

A fucking paradise.

As he inched deeper, her brow furrowed and her fingers dug into her breasts. Her eyes sparkled.

"Oh my God," she whispered when he had nearly pushed his entire length into her arse.

She gasped when his cock flexed inside her.

"How does my pet like getting her arse filled?" he inquired, thinking how beautiful she looked just now.

"A lot," she murmured.

If she were more experienced with anal sex, he would have grabbed the headboard behind her and thrust into her like there was no tomorrow. Instead, he moved slowly, all the while teasing her clit. He grunted when he had buried himself to the hilt.

"Your arse feels so fucking amazing," he told her, pinning her with his stare.

She stared back. "Make me come."

He didn't care that it wasn't in the form of a question. He was happy to oblige, gently drawing his cock out, then sinking back in. He took one of her hands and moved it to her clit, freeing his hands so he could plant them beside her and cover more of her body with his.

"Oh, God, yes," she exhaled. "I'm g-going to come."

He captured her lips, muffling her cries. Minutes

later, he drank in her scream as she erupted into spasms. He only had to spear into her a few times before his own climax sent quakes throughout his body, culminating in a tsunami as he poured himself into her.

Greater euphoria was not possible. This was as good as it gets.

She was as good as it gets.

*****

"What? There's more?" she mumbled when he slid beneath her body with the Womanizer in hand.

"I said we're going to top ten orgasms," he replied, spreading her folds before turning on the device.

"Oh my God," she gasped when it sucked at her clit.

Minutes later, she was begging fast. "Please may I come? Oh, Jesus!"

He turned up the setting.

"Please!"

"Hang on," he denied.

"Please, please, please..."

He could tell she wouldn't be able to hold back much longer.

"Pleeeease!"

"Okay, now."

She bucked atop him, wailing, and would have sat up if he hadn't held her down.

"Okay, I came," she said through chattering teeth.

"Once more."

"No!"

He knew her clit was extremely sensitive, but she could do it. "Dig deep for me, pet."

She tried to squirm away, but he shifted his grip to her throat. That stilled her somewhat. She made a half-sob and grabbed his arm, digging her nails painfully into him.

"It's there," he assured her. "Come for me."

"Fuck," she cried, her body writhing, tensing.

"Work with me."

Her pants and cries of distress turned to groans and cries of pleasure. The convulsions were larger the second time, the screaming louder. The sadist in him would have left the device attached to her poor clit, but he backed off the setting till the suction gave way.

She rolled off him but continued to tremble. He pulled her into his arms and kissed her temple. He savored the softness of her body against him, the weight of her head on his shoulder, her breath on his chest.

He didn't want to leave her. He wanted to take her back to his place, but he had to fly to Vancouver in the morning to evaluate a project there and meet with possible partners. So it was best that he take her back to her own place.

"You got your childcare center and new basketball courts," he praised.

She looked ready to fall asleep but smiled. "Where is the childcare center going to be?"

"I don't know," he admitted. "There's actually an ideal spot in Chinatown, but the property owner is being a wanker, trying to hold out for a ridiculous asking price."

She snuggled into him. "I'm sure you'll figure out something."

He held her tighter. "I have to leave town in the morning, but I'll be back Friday night."

"I'm having dinner with my folks Friday night."

"Then I'll pick you up Saturday at ten."

"In the morning?"

"I thought maybe you'd want to go to the Stanford football game with me."

She started and opened her eyes. "Really?"

"I happen to have tickets. Fifty-yard line."

She popped up on an elbow. "What's the catch? You want to fuck my arse again?"

"Yes to the second question, and the answer to the first is there's no catch. Just come watch the game with me. Unless you don't like football."

"Are you kidding? I'd love to go!"

Her response was just what he had hoped for. He cupped the side of her face and pulled her into a kiss.

"You're being straight with me?" she inquired when he released her. "I don't have to give up anything to go?"

"Babe, I'm fucking you either way. I don't need football tickets for that."

She seemed to contemplate if there was anything she might be missing. "Okay. Cool. I still think you're an asshole, though."

But she no longer sounded mad at him.

"I know," he said. "Doesn't bother me a bit, love."

It wasn't entirely true. He wondered if, in fact, it would be possible for her to love a man she deemed an asshole?

Chapter Twenty-Six

The alarm went off, and Kimani leaped out of bed, thinking that she was going to be late for work, then realizing she didn't have a job to go to anymore.

And that was because of Ben.

A man who had devastated her body last night. She was sore in a lot of places, especially between her legs, the interior parts that his cock had decimated. Yet she relished the sensation. Though she was glad he would be out of country, giving her a reprieve, she did look forward to his return.

"Your Asian hottie must be back in the picture," Keisha remarked after Kimani agreed to Fulani braids.

"Just for three days," Kimani admitted as she leaned back over a sink for Keisha to wash her hair. "This is more of an I'm-starting-a-new-chapter-in-my-life hairdo."

"Yeah? What's the new chapter?"

"Unemployment."

"Oh no. You serious?"

"I've got a severance package, so I'm good for a while," Kimani replied. *Though I should probably be saving my money instead of blowing it on fancy braids.*

"You'll find a new job. Maybe better than the one you had."

"Maybe."

"I'm sorry, girl. My uncle works for the waste management company. Maybe they have an opening in their office."

"Thanks. I'm sure I'll find something."

"That's right. You got those degrees from Stanford and Cal."

Wanting to keep the conversation on the lighter side, Kimani didn't tell Keisha that the field of journalism wasn't easy, no matter what schools one went to. She did, however, feel the need to confide her conflicting emotions to someone, and Keisha wouldn't let her get away with anything.

"I knew my position at the *Tribune* probably wasn't going to last," Kimani said. "The paper was probably going to close regardless, so it shouldn't matter that I lost my job because of him."

"Who?"

"Ben. The 'Asian hottie.'"

Keisha, working in the leave-in conditioner, stopped. "How's that?"

"He bought the *Tribune* and shut it down. I guess I shouldn't be mad because I got a more generous severance package, when I could have gotten nothing if the paper had simply run out of money."

"He know you were working there?"

"He did."

"Is he helping you find a new job?"

"No." *But I did get a childcare center and new basketball courts out of him.*

"Then why are you seeing the guy?"

"Because I lost a game of twenty-one."

Keisha raised an eyebrow. "What now?"

"We had a bet on the game. If I lost, I had to see him for three days."

"And by 'see him,' you mean have sex with him."

Couldn't get anything past Keisha, Kimani thought to herself.

"Pretty much," Kimani acknowledged.

"And I take it this Ben is good in bed."

You don't know the half of it. Aloud, Kimani said, "The thing is, I *am* upset that he shut down the paper."

"You said the paper was going to close anyway."

"I see that as dying a natural death. What he did was a gunshot to the head."

Keisha started brushing out any tangles. "So why'd he do it?"

"He had reasons—legit reasons—but, still, he didn't have to do what he did."

"If he had legit reasons, why are you being so hard on him?"

"I don't know. Because he thinks he can do whatever the hell he wants and get whatever the hell he wants 'cause he has the financial resources."

"How rich is this guy?"

"As an individual, I'm not sure. According to *Forbes*, the family is worth over ten billion."

"If you get tired of this guy, you send him my way."

"Just 'cause he has money?"

"And you said he has it going on in bed."

"I didn't say that, exactly."

"You didn't have to."

Kimani blushed.

"What more do you need in a guy? Hell, if he has ten billion dollars and a halfway decent ass—he has a good ass, right? I can't take flabby pale asses."

"He has a killer ass."

"Then what's your problem?"

"I have a problem with how he shoves his weight around 'cause he has money."

"That's the way of the world, honey. If you've got it, why not flaunt it? Don't resent him for what the good Lord gave him."

"There are lots of bad people whom the good Lord has granted riches to."

"Is he one of them?"

"No, but that doesn't make him any more deserving."

"Are you trying to right all that's unfair?"

"I can try to do my part."

Using the end of a rat-tail comb, Keisha began to part the hair in rows. "So what is it you're trying to do? Deny him your love so that he doesn't get to have it all?"

Kimani made a face. "Who said anything about love?"

"You're not fooling me, girl. See, you brainy types think you can reason or talk through anything, but your feelings—they're obvious anyway."

"I have *mixed* feelings about him."

"That's 'cause your brain is getting in the way, trying to make things more complicated than they really are."

Kimani was silent in thought. Her basketball coach had once advised her not to overthink things. Trust your instincts and let it flow, her coach had said.

"He only wants me for three days," Kimani said, "then he's probably back off to China or wherever."

"Then make the most of your three days, girl."

Kimani met Keisha's look in the mirror and smiled. "I should pay you for doing more than my hair."

"Mmm-hmm. Damn right. Keisha won't steer you wrong *and* you get super-sexy braids to boot."

*****

Sporting her new braided swoop, Kimani stopped by Gordon's campaign headquarters. She didn't feel like job hunting just yet.

"Kimani, I want to thank you again for putting together that event," Gordon said to her. "I got a call from East Oakland Kids, and they couldn't be happier. They even got an anonymous donation of ten thousand dollars today!"

Kimani smiled. "That's great!"

"And Anthony tells me you're a top-notch precinct walker. If I get elected, would you want a job at City Hall?"

"Oh wow. Umm..."

"I heard the *Tribune* closed."

Kimani wondered if Ben had told his uncle. Probably not. Gordon didn't seem like the kind of guy who would be okay with a move like that. Not that Ben wouldn't do it anyway, with or without his uncle's approval.

"I *am* in the market for a job," Kimani said, "and working for you would be an honor."

"The honor would be mine. So that's a 'yes?'"

"For now. I haven't had a chance to see what's out there in the field of journalism."

Gordon nodded. "You just let me know when. My chances of winning have improved today. Dawson Chang just came out with his endorsement."

"That's great news, too," Kimani said, surprised that everything had happened so fast. She was curious if Ben had anything to do with it, but she didn't want to take away from the possibility that Gordon had earned the endorsement on his own merits.

Later that day, Kimani met up Ron and Robin for drinks where Marissa worked. Ron and Robin were partially recovered and acclimating to their new state of unemployment.

"Do we get to collect unemployment insurance after our severance package ends?" Ron asked.

"Maybe that's one of the questions Human Resources will answer at the employee meeting on Friday," Robin said.

"Where's this meeting again?"

"Some law office downtown. Jones and Finch."

Kimani recalled the moment she had discovered that Ben was behind the *Tribune's* closure. Had she been too self-righteous in her anger?

"Well, I say we make the most of our unemployment," Ron said. "I'm going to take a trip to Costa Rica."

"I already threw a pity party for myself and spent all of yesterday shopping," Robin said, displaying her new handbag.

"What about you, Taylor?"

"I got these braids," Kimani answered.

Robin fingered one of the beads. "Your braids are gorgeous. I wish I could get my hair done like this, but I don't want to be accused of cultural appropriation."

"If it makes you happy—"

Robin shook her head. "We can't always do what makes us happy."

"I bet I'd look pretty hot in Fulani braids," Ron joked.

They ended their evening with a toast to unemployment.

"I might be home late," Marissa told Kimani as she got ready to leave. "Miguel's going to be at The Lair."

"Oh, well, have fun." Kimani gave her roommate a wink and hug. "You going to be okay returning home alone?"

"Miguel promised to take me home. I told him about the break-in. What about you? It's kind of late."

"The police had a talk with Jake, so I don't think he's going to try to pull anything—at least not for a while."

But she was wrong.

After getting dropped off in front of her house, someone came up behind her just as she was about to unlock the door.

"Excuse me, buddy," she heard behind her.

Before she could turn around, she was shoved face first into the door. Pain exploded at her forehead, and her vision blurred. Two perpetrators were fighting each other, then it seemed a third appeared. At first, she was too shocked and disoriented to do anything. A gun went off, jolting her enough to scream, but a gruff hand covered her mouth and slammed the back of her head to the door. She slumped to the ground.

Chapter Twenty-Seven

Bataar didn't have to say anything before Ben knew that something was wrong. Bataar wouldn't knock on Ben's hotel room at this hour of night unless he had something important to say.

"Chin's been shot," Bataar informed. "And Moe's not answering his phone."

Ben felt his veins turn cold. "Kimani."

Bataar was silent for one second too long. This had just gone from bad to worse.

"Chin managed to get in his car to tail Jake," Bataar continued, "but he had to pull over because he was losing too much blood."

Ben felt a vein explode. "So we don't know where she is?!"

"Bill's on his way to Kimani's home, which is where Moe's cell locater is signaling, and Chin already called 9-1-1," Bataar said, rubbing his jaw.

Shit. A flight back to San Francisco would take at least two and a half hours.

"Your jet is being readied," Bataar said.

Not bothering to pack, Ben grabbed his mobile, threw on his shoes, and strode out. A gun meant this wasn't about a little act of intimidation. Fucking Jake!

"We had two guys at the scene, and we couldn't

stop Jake?" Ben thundered.

"Vince was there. And Chin didn't think he needed to have his piece on him."

Ben took a breath to keep his blood pressure from going through the roof. He had to keep his emotions in check if he was going to think clearly. "How was she?"

"A little banged up. Chin couldn't tell for sure."

"How far did he follow Jake?"

"Somewhere outside Santa Rosa."

Sonoma County. Where could they be headed?

"The cabin," Ben answered himself out loud. "That's probably where they're headed. Call the Trinity County Sherriff's office. And have Bill meet up with us."

"What about Moe?"

"The emergency responders can help him more than Bill can. We're going to need a car to meet us at Weaverville in case we can't get one at this hour."

Flying into Weaverville would be shorter than flying into San Francisco. Ben only hoped he could get there in time.

Chapter Twenty-Eight

Kimani stood at the edge of a pier overlooking dark ocean waters beneath a moonless sky. Rope encircled her body, pinning her arms to her sides and her legs together.

"Come on, pet," Ben called to her from where he treaded water.

She observed the choppy waves with doubt.

"Don't make me come and get you," he warned.

She looked from the water into his eyes, which she desperately tried to read, but they were also dark. She wasn't sure why she didn't explain that she couldn't swim when she was all tied up. She supposed it was obvious.

Ben continued to tread water. He seemed at ease, but then, he didn't have his hands tied.

Though she couldn't tell in the dark, it seemed his expression softened.

"Trust me."

With the grip of fear still about her, she jumped.

Water splashed over her. She coughed. Her head hurt.

"Wakey, wakey, slut."

Kimani opened her eyes. She wanted to wipe away the droplets in her eyes, but rope still bound her. She felt wet, but she wasn't in the ocean.

A hand slapped the side of her face. Had she drowned? Was Ben trying to revive her?

"I said to wake the fuck up, slut!"

She felt thumbs at her eyes, pulling her eyelids up.

The face of Jake Whitehurst came into view.

"That's better," he said.

She tried to turn her head away from the faint spray of his spit, but he caught her jaw roughly.

"Look at me when I'm talking to you," he growled, slapping her once more.

Her mind started to piece together her situation, and it wasn't good. She remembered being accosted on her front doorstep, a scuffle, darkness, the hum of a car, her immobility. She had been dreaming just now but awoke to a nightmare.

"You're such a bad slut," he spit. "All that time with Benji boy, and you haven't learned a damn thing. Maybe I got it wrong. Maybe *he* was the pussy. Is that right?"

Despite the throbbing of her head, she was able to focus on Jake and take in her surroundings. She was tied to a chair. They seemed to be alone. Where?

She recognized the windowless room with the single lightbulb overhead. It was where she and her peers from the Scarlet Auction had slept. Jake's cabin in Trinity County.

She tried to stifle the panic rising in her throat. Even if she could escape outside, there wouldn't be anyone to run to for miles.

Where was her cellphone? Where was his? She

looked him over but didn't see anything.

"Checking me out, slut?" he asked with a grin. "This is what a real Dom looks like. I'm gonna show you how it's *really* done."

She wondered if it was still night or had it turned to day? If the latter, then Marissa would have noticed her missing. Maybe she would have called the police, but would they consider her a missing person if it hadn't been twenty-four hours yet?

She couldn't count on anyone coming to her aid. She had no idea what Jake intended, if he just meant to bully her or if he was capable of murder, but she had to stall him somehow.

"What happened?" she asked, even though she knew the answer.

"So you're incompetent *and* stupid. Man, you people were better off on the plantations."

She regretted the times she had called Ben an asshole. Jake Whitehurst and his kind were the real assholes.

"What's the matter? Don't like what I said?" he sneered. "It's what the majority of this country believes, even if they're too nice to say it out loud. So you go right on and do your protesting shit. The truth is—people don't give a rat's ass."

Stay calm, Kimani. You just want to make it out alive.

"What is it you want, Jake?" she asked, subtly trying to test out her bonds and see if there was a loose end somewhere.

He smirked, which made him look even nastier, even though someone who didn't know him would consider him extremely good-looking. "I want that blow job you owe me."

She tried not recoil in disgust. "I owe you a blow job?"

He unzipped his black jeans and pulled out his penis. "You were lucky Claire was up to the task that first night. I got cheated."

Kimani tried not to look at his dick because doing so made her stomach turn over. "Ben wanted his money back?"

"Surprisingly, he didn't ask for it back. Probably thought he owed it to me for breaking Vince's arm. But two hundred thousand dollars doesn't come close to making up for what I had to go through."

Her eyes widened in disbelief. "*You're* the victim?"

"Yeah. Some bitch sports agent found out I pled out on an assault charge and pulled that MeToo shit, telling people I attack women. I lost two potential clients on account of cunts like her. And *you*. Women like you are so fucked up. You dig BDSM and rape fantasies, but when it happens for real, you wanna make men pay for your own messed-up shit. Deep down you want it, but you buy into that feminist shit that you're not supposed to, so you take it out on men. So, hell yeah, I'm the victim here!"

There was no use explaining to someone like Jake the difference between fantasy and reality, or that BDSM done right involved a lot of consent.

Jake stroked his cock to semi-erectness. "So this blow job is on behalf of all men who have had to put up with cunts like you."

Keep him talking.

"Are you saying all men are innocent?"

"They haven't been proven guilty. But these days, they're automatically guilty just because some stupid slut says a guy put the moves on her."

"That didn't happen with the most recent Supreme Court nomination. He was presumed innocent by a majority of the Senate."

"Yeah, but he got raked over the coals. Someone owes him a helluva blow job."

His penis was inches from her face.

Lord, please don't make me have to taste his junk.

As if in answer to her prayer, there was a knock at the door.

"What?" Jake growled.

"Claire's here," Vince said from the other side.

"What the fuck?"

"She said you told her you'd be at the lake this weekend, and she decided to surprise you."

"Fuck! I never confirmed to her I was going." Jake stuffed his penis back in his jeans and went to open the door. "She drive herself up? What the hell?"

Vince didn't bother looking over at Kimani. "What should I do with her?"

"Fuck. I fucking hate blonds."

Jake stepped out and slammed the door behind him. Kimani heard him stomping up the stairs.

Claire was here! She wasn't alone with Jake. Kimani felt a ray of hope. Though Claire hadn't proved too helpful last time, her presence was better than none.

Kimani could see a lot of anger and hate in Jake. Was it enough to be deadly? She had to assume the possibility was there. Either way, she had to get out of here before discovering the answer.

Chapter Twenty-Nine

"The cops said they didn't find anyone at the cabin," Bataar said.

They were in Ben's jet en route to Weaverville.

"Jake must not have made it there yet," Ben said. "Have them go back."

Shit. A lot could happen before the sheriff's deputy made it back to the cabin. If they even agreed to go check again.

As Bataar waited for the county sheriff's office to pick up his call, he added, "Bill's been driving nearly a hundred miles an hour, but we'll still beat him there. He'll meet us at the cabin."

Bataar had secured a car, having found a saloon in Weaverville that was open and bribing the owner with a thousand dollars if he could meet them at the airport and let them borrow his car.

Ben prayed he was right that Jake was headed to his lakeside cabin. Because if he wasn't...or he didn't make it on time...

Chapter Thirty

Twenty or so minutes had passed by, and Kimani had come up with nothing, no strategy for escape. She had spent a good part of her time trying to assess how much danger she was in and trying not to panic. She knew Jake could get violent, and after what he had been through, he probably hated her now more than ever.

But she did have one helpful thought—if she could get her hands free, she stood a better chance. And maybe the only way she could do that was to play the part he wanted. Appease him long enough to catch him off guard.

She shuddered. She'd rather eat vomit than have to pander to Jake, but she didn't have much of a choice.

She looked around the room to see if anything could be used as a weapon but found nothing. At least she had a strategy now.

"Time for nappy hoes to be fed," Jake announced as he entered and closed the door behind him.

She knew what he intended for a meal and wanted to retch. Noticing he had a scotch in hand, she wondered how much he'd had to drink, and if his drinking was a good thing or a bad thing. The alcohol could impair him or it could make him more violent and lose control.

She also noticed that the lock hadn't actually engaged and the door slid open a crack.

Excitement shot up her spine. She prayed Jake didn't notice. Maybe she could scream for help? Maybe Claire was in the cabin and could hear her? But if not, she would only upset Jake, and who knew what he might do. She decided to keep the screaming in her back pocket until she had a better assessment of whether or not it could be useful.

"Let's see how good you give head," Jake snickered. "You got them big-ass lips. Maybe they're good for something."

Unzipping his fly with one hand, he pulled out his penis and stroked himself.

How was she going to get him to untie her? she wondered. Was there a way to delay the blow job he wanted?

He smeared the tip of his penis over her lips, and her whole body recoiled in horror. She suppressed painful feelings of helplessness and violation. She needed to do what she needed to do.

"Come on, slut," he said, "you know you want it. Nothing better than a big white cock, right?"

If it weren't for the grave situation she was in, she might have retorted that it was complexes around big white cocks that led to so many problems in the world, both current and historical.

"What's the matter?" Jake snarled. "You like small chinky dicks better?"

She stared at his member. Her stomach churned.

"Can I at least go to the bathroom first?" she asked. "I haven't gone since—"

In the split second it took for her to see his fist raised, she reacted, twisting her body to try to get away from his punch. It glanced off her cheek, and the floor struck her other cheek when she fell over.

"Jake, would you want—"

Through the haze of pain, Kimani heard, then saw Claire at the threshold.

Claire stared at them with a puzzled expression.

"I thought you were taking a fucking bath," Jake growled.

"I came to see if you wanted to take one with me," Claire replied, still dumbfounded by what she had stumbled across.

"Claire, call 9-1-1!" Kimani told her.

Claire blinked several times, then turned to head back upstairs. She must have heard the panic in Kimani's voice. But Jake had covered the distance and, grabbing Claire by the hair, dragged her into the room.

"You stupid bitch," Jake spat, shaking her. "I never told you to come up here! But since you're here, I'll let you have the first taste."

After pushing her to her knees, he wagged his penis in front of her.

"Go on, slut."

Claire started to tear up. He smacked her hard across the face, then took a sip of the drink he still held.

"What's the matter with you bitches?" he asked. He

grabbed her long golden hair again to pull her back up to her knees. "Open up, Slut #1. Or were you Slut #2?"

Crying, Claire was trembling too hard to do much. He pinched her nose, forcing her to breathe through her mouth, and shoved himself into her. She gagged immediately.

"Stupid fucking bitch," he muttered before hitting her and knocking her to the floor.

She cried harder.

"Look," Kimani said to Jake, "I'll do whatever the hell you want. You want me to suck you off? I'll suck you off real good. Just don't hurt us."

Jake smiled. "Now that's more like it."

"You want to see what I can do with my hands while I go down on you? Guys like it when I tug their balls at the same time I suck their cock. I finger the perineum nice and good. And it's fucking amazing with a finger up your ass at the same time. You ever feel how good that is?"

Jake contemplated the idea. "You better not try anything or I'll beat the shit out of you both."

Claire sobbed louder.

Jake turned to her. "Shut up!"

Still holding his scotch somehow, he loosened the rope enough for Kimani to get out. He pulled her to her knees and presented his dick.

"This better be as good as you say it is," he spat.

She glanced over at Claire, who had curled into a fetal position. She was on her own, Kimani assessed.

"Get on with it, bitch, or I'll rip these braids off

your head," Jake threatened, grabbing her hair.

She took a hold of his member, contemplating the wisdom of biting it. Maybe if she got him to the point of coming and bit him then, he wouldn't be able to react fast enough to hit her.

Trying not to wonder if he had any STDs, she wrapped her lips over his tip. She watched him take a sip of his drink—and had an idea. She came off his penis and loosened her hold...

When he lowered his drink, she shoved the pad of her palm to the bottom of the glass, splashing the contents into his face.

He roared when the alcohol stung his eyes. As he rubbed his eyes, she ran to the chair, picked it up, and slammed it into him, knocking him to the ground.

"Run!" Kimani yelled at Claire.

Claire managed to scramble to her feet. Kimani turned and slammed into something hard.

Vince.

"What the hell—" he began.

He grabbed Kimani and pulled out his gun. Claire screamed.

When he looked in her direction, Kimani, recalling a self-defense move, stepped closer to Vince and head-butted him in the chin.

He stumbled backward. His hand hit the doorframe, dislodging the gun, which skidded over to Claire's feet.

"Pick it up!" Kimani cried.

Though shaking violently, Claire got the gun,

pointing it at Vince as he scrambled toward her.

"Give me the gun, sweetheart," Vince said. "You don't want to hurt anyone."

Kimani ran over to Claire and tried to take the gun, but Claire's hands seemed frozen in place, so she put her hands over Claire's. Adrenaline flowed in her veins.

At any moment, Claire might accidentally pull the trigger. Hell, at any moment, she might do the same.

"I want a phone," Kimani said to the two men. "Which of you two has a phone?"

"There's no cell coverage here," Jake sneered from where he half knelt.

"Bullshit." She remembered having made a call on Ben's cellphone.

While she contemplated whether or not she and Claire should just make a run for it, she heard tires squealing outside. Was it the police? But how would they know to come? Did Jake have more than Vince working for him?

Thinking it might be the latter, Kimani grabbed Claire. "Let's go!"

She managed to take the gun from Claire as they dashed up the stairs, with Jake and Vince not far behind.

The front door to the cabin swung open. Kimani brought the gun up.

"Stop or I'll shoot!" she exclaimed.

She found herself looking into the end of another gun barrel.

"Kimani!"

Ben? Was she hearing correctly?

And then she saw him. The most welcome sight in the world.

He stepped from behind Bataar, grabbed her arm and, yanking her past his body, decked Vince, who had come up behind her.

Bataar caught her and spun her behind him. He then pulled Claire out of the house, his gun trained on Vince. Ben turned and saw Jake, who was halfway up the stairs, and chased him back down.

"Kimani!" Bataar yelled when she ran after Ben.

She entered the basement in time to see Ben throw Jake against the wall.

"I was just—" Jake objected before Ben slammed him into the wall a second time.

"Ben!" Kimani shouted.

Jake slid to the ground.

"What are you doing?" she asked, racing over.

"Beating the shit out of him for you," Ben said between heavy breaths.

"I don't need you to do that," she said. She handed him the gun. "I'll do it myself."

Kimani kicked Jake as hard as she could in the ribs. "That's for all the cunts in the world."

She aimed her next kick at his groin. Jake curled his body and grabbed his crotch with an agonized groan. Kimani glanced over at Ben.

He stared at her intently. "God, I'm in love."

Turning back to Jake, he delivered a swift kick to Jake's face.

"Fuck! My nose!" Jake screamed as blood gushed over him.

Ben aimed the gun at him.

"Ben!" Kimani screamed, grabbing his arm.

"You want this fucker to live?" Ben asked, his tone icy and serious.

"I don't want *you* to go to prison." She pleaded with every nerve in her body. "Jesus, I still owe you two days."

His expression softened. "Yeah, you do."

He lowered the gun. With his thumb, he wiped the blood from her bottom lip. She hadn't even realized she had sustained a cut there till now. His gaze swept over the rest of her, noticing the bruise on her forehead.

His pupils constricted, and his eyes darkened. "What did he do to you?"

Not wanting to go into detail for fear that Ben might take justice into his own hands, she said, "Nothing. You came just in time. How did you know we were here? I thought you were in Vancouver?"

"Bataar had a guy on Jake...and a bodyguard on you."

"A what?"

"Are you sure you're okay?"

"Yeah, but maybe we should check on Claire."

They left Jake in the basement and locked the door. Upstairs, another car had pulled up. A man emerged, whom Kimani recognized as the man who had given her a lift back to the campaign headquarters the day she'd found out Ben was behind the closure of the *Tribune*.

"That's Bill. He was your daytime bodyguard," Ben explained.

She raised her brows. "I had a nighttime bodyguard, too?"

"Moe."

Bataar looked at them from where he was standing guard over Vince, whom he had lying face down in the foyer with his hands behind his back. "Moe's going to be okay. He sustained a minor concussion. And Chin found his way to the hospital."

"Who's Chin?" she asked.

"The guy we had on Jake," Ben explained.

Claire was sitting on the doorstep, shivering and in a daze, her cheeks stained with mascara. Ben took off his jacket and put it around her shoulders. Kimani was about to sit down next to her, but Ben grabbed her. He looked her over again, and there was an edge to his voice when he spoke.

"When you get checked by the doctor, and if I find out you fucking lied about what Jake—"

"Then you get to punish me," she interrupted. She made her voice sultry. "I hope you punish me good, Master."

Chapter Thirty-One

"**P**unish me good, Master."

It was music to his ears. Ben smiled as he circled Kimani. In his playroom, he had set three thick bamboo poles in a tripod as if to form the frame for a teepee. From the center, where he had tied the poles together with a clove hitch, Kimani dangled by her arms near the floor. Her right ankle was tied to the bottom of one pole while her other was pulled asymmetrically up toward another pole, forcing her thighs open. She had on one of his button-down shirts that she'd knotted at the waist. The rest of her was as naked as sin.

Squatting down, he undid the buttons of her top. Slipping a hand into the garment, he squeezed a breast and tugged on an already-erect nipple.

"Mmmm," he murmured.

He pinched the nipple, making her strain against her bonds. He pulled the top open to expose both breasts, then caressed each of the areolas and teased the nipples to further hardness.

Crop in hand, he landed the end of the implement on her chest. She grunted. He struck the side of her breast. She gasped. He smacked her breast dead center. She cried out.

"Thank you, Master," she whimpered.

He slapped her other breast with his hand before applying the crop. She yelped and writhed beneath the tripod. Rising to his feet, he tapped the crop along her midsection to her thighs. He slapped the crop on an inner thigh, making her jump. Standing in front of her, he admired the bare and supple folds between her legs. Earlier, he had taken a razor and trimmed the curls at her mound.

"Such a pretty pussy," he complimented.

Squatting down again, he caressed the smooth flesh and toyed with her clit, encouraging it to emerge and swell. She purred as she watched him intently. Their gazes met over the hills and valley of her body. Her stare made his cock harden against his pants.

He had come home to his place in Pacific Heights from his office with the intention of taking Kimani out to dinner, but she had looked utterly too hot in his shirt, sans a bra, and a pair of his basketball shorts that looked ready to fall off her hips.

She hadn't wanted to stay at his place initially, but since coming back from Trinity County, he had refused to let Kimani out of his sight for the first few days. Even though Jake and Vince, who had both been denied bail, were an unlikely threat and Bataar was on duty as her primary security, Ben didn't trust anyone.

He drew the moisture between her folds to her clit and fondled her till she groaned.

"Can I come, Sir?"

"This being a punishment, what do you think the answer is?" he replied.

She let her head fall back. "Ugh."

He tapped the crop up the inside of one thigh and down the other, then slapped it on the bottom of her raised foot. She cried out.

"Hold the crop," he instructed, placing it between her teeth. "Make sure you don't drop it."

He rolled up the sleeves of his dress shirt and, from a nearby table, selected a small wooden stick with a point at the end, almost like a pencil. He grasped her foot and ran the point down the arch of her foot. She bit down harder on the crop. Her body writhed forcefully, tugging against her bonds. He poked the bottom of her foot with the stick, then dragged it up the arch. She screamed around the crop.

Finished, he kissed the bottom of her foot.

"I don't know that I'll ever like bastinado," she said between difficult breaths after he had removed the crop from her mouth.

"Then we'll go back to the crop."

He slapped it over her belly, against her side, and over her twat.

"Ow!" she cried.

He landed it sharply on an outer thigh, the side of a buttock, and between her legs again.

"Shit!"

The bamboo poles shook with her jerking. He gave her a reprieve. With her head hanging back, she stared the ceiling.

When he moved, her head snapped up. She was on alert again, her gaze following him so that she might guess where he would strike next.

He didn't, choosing instead to exchange the crop for a classic teardrop butt plug with a flared handle. Kneeling before her, he rubbed the plug along her slit, collecting her juices. Her eyelashes fluttered as he slid it against her clit. He dipped the plug into her to lubricate it further. She moaned as he fucked her with the plug for a bit before pulling it out and nestling the tip at the other pink opening below. Some of her moisture had already dripped there. He rested his other hand on her pubic bone and thumbed her clit before inserting the tip into her bottom hole.

"You've got to keep it in if you want to come later," he told her, pushing more of the plug in and finding some resistance.

"Yes, Sir."

He let the plug rest halfway so her body could adjust to the foreign object. Lowering his head, he tongued her clit.

"Jesus," she moaned when he starting going to town on her.

He pushed the plug all the way in till her sphincter closed around the neck of the plug. He held it in place so that her muscle contractions wouldn't expel the plug.

"Keep it in," he reminded her.

Her brows knit it concentration as she forced her body to accept the plug. Letting go of the handle, he sat back to admire the crystal jewelry at the end of the plug.

"Good pet," he praised before sinking two digits into her twat.

"Oh, God," she groaned. "That feels so good, Master."

He smiled and worked her till she was squirming and panting.

"Can I please, please come?" she murmured, her brow intensely furrowed.

"Am I nice guy?" he teased.

"Yes! You're such a nice Master. You're the nicest fucking guy around."

"You don't really believe that, do you, pet?"

She flushed.

"For lying, I might make you wear the plug all day tomorrow."

She frowned.

"But I *will* let you come right now. Because I'm not a complete arsehole."

She brightened. His fingers hit all the right spots inside her.

"Ohhhh..." She grimaced.

"Are you going to come for me, pet?"

"Y-Yes, Sir."

"Are you?"

"Yes!"

Her answer devolved into a sob as she lost control of her limbs. The muscles inside her clamped down on his digits while her body bucked and shook. It was an amazing sight. One he would never tire of.

After the quaking of her body had settled, he undid

his pants and pulled out his eager cock. He slapped his cock against her flesh and rubbed it along her clit. He wanted nothing more than to feel her flesh to flesh, to spill himself into her, implant his seed in her womb, but he didn't want her to have to worry about taking a morning-after pill, so he slid on a condom before sinking himself into her.

Her eyes flew open at being filled in both holes. He, too, could feel the presence of the plug.

"God, you're fucking marvelous," he said to her.

"So are you, Master."

He grunted. He couldn't decide if he wanted to fuck her because he couldn't contain how much his body went crazy for her, or make love to her because he wanted to show he was worthy of her affection. He rolled his hips gently as he considered which it would be. She responded, trying to move her hips in rhythm to his, clenching down on his member, making him want to fuck hard. But he held off on letting the beast loose.

She had been banged up enough by Jake. The bruise on her forehead had receded but wasn't fully gone.

He watched her every breath, every blink of the eye, every tremor of the body. Reaching for a breast, he massaged the orb as he paced himself with the thrusting, wanting to draw out her pleasure as well as his own. When she started to move a little too much, like she wanted to do the fucking, he slapped the breast.

"Just sit back and enjoy this one," he advised.

Her eyes closed and her body relaxed. Holding on to her legs, he thrust into the most delicious heat he had ever known. She shivered with each withdrawal and groaned as he dove back in.

"Can I come?" she remembered to ask.

"You had better."

Within minutes, her body was straining, arching, shaking. He pumped himself deep, then pulled out quickly. Her body released a stream of wetness. He shoved himself back in, bucked several times, and yanked his cock out. She was a mess of rattled nerves, squirting, cursing, and crying. It was exactly how he liked her.

After shedding his clothes, he removed the plug and untied her from the poles. Wrapping her in his arms, he carried her to the bed. As soon as he sat down with her on his lap, she pushed him down to the bed and crushed her lips atop his, mauling him with her mouth.

Hot damn.

Grabbing the back of her head, he kissed her back. She slid her body over his, shoving parts of herself at his cock.

"You want to fuck me, don't you?" he murmured against her lips.

"May I, Master?" she asked coyly.

He laughed at her fake demureness. "All right, pet. Fuck me."

She straddled him and sank down on his cock.

Bloody. Fuck.

He forced him to stay still to see how she would ride him. She ground herself into his pelvis, rubbing her wetness all over him. Then she pushed herself up his shaft, tightening about him at the same time. Pleasure percolated up and down his cock and tingled down his legs. She had strong thighs and was able to pump herself up and down easily. He watched her breasts bounce and groped one.

She found that if she rode him at a slight angle, her own pleasure increased. Perspiration glowed upon her skin, and the arousal in her face made his balls boil in excitement. It was hard for him to stay out of the action, so he grabbed her hips, and bucked himself into her. She gasped loudly at being speared so forcefully. He eased his thrusts.

"Come on, pet. Come for me."

Her paroxysm would have toppled her from him if he hadn't been holding on to her. He shoved himself deep and fast, making her teeth chatter, till he exploded in glory. He roared as the tension in his body burst through his erection, sending waves of rapture behind it, rippling from his head to his toes. The sensation overwhelmed him, and he had to close his eyes to shut out unwanted stimulation. He lie bathed in jaw-dropping bliss, trying to find his breath as Kimani collapsed over him.

He wrapped his arms about her, holding her close as his member throbbed inside of her. After they had lain in quiet for several minutes, he kissed her temple and asked if she wanted to go out for dinner.

"How about that noodle place in Chinatown, the place you took me to before?" she suggested. "I feel like Chinese."

"Whatever you want. If you feel like French, there's a great little place in the Rue Cler."

She pushed herself up to look into his face. "I have an appointment with the therapist in the morning."

The therapist. His anger rose as he wondered how long she would have to be in therapy to work out the trauma. He should have killed Jake when he'd had the chance. Now she still had to see the bastard in court.

"And Ms. Clarkson wants to talk with me again," Kimani added as she idly circled her finger over his nipple. "Thanks to the Scarlet Auction documents you gave her, she feels she has a strong case. They've subpoenaed a lot of people now, not just Claire. And Claire's not going to defend anyone this time."

"They better not cut Jake too good a deal," Ben said grimly.

Jake had offered to spill the goods on the Scarlet Auction, with whom he had coordinated to intimidate Kimani. It was someone from the Scarlet Auction who had broken into her home and taken her computer.

"Ms. Clarkson seems like a hard-ass," Kimani replied.

Ben imagined a lot of people considered Ms. Clarkson a bitch, and he hadn't been taken with her at the beginning, but now he was glad Ms. Clarkson was on the case. Maybe the world could use more hard-charging women.

"Hey, it's gonna be okay," Kimani said.

He looked at her in surprise. After all that she had been through, she was trying to comfort *him*? He pulled her in closer.

"We should get you to bed early," he said. "You've also got work tomorrow."

"I finished most of the details for Gordon's campaign rally yesterday."

"I meant you have a job to go to."

She tilted her head. "I don't have a job because some overbearing billionaire shut down the paper I worked at."

"Yeah, well, I changed my mind."

She stared at him with eyes agog. He smiled to himself. He was going to see that look again when he told her he had tickets to the Warriors' opening night.

"Oh my God, I love you," she squeaked—then backpedaled as she seemed to decide it was too good to be true.

Still, the words rang in his ears and caused his breath to stop.

"But," she said, "you're just going to lose more money keeping the paper open."

"Maybe I can take a page from Bezos' playbook," he said, referring to the acquisition of the *The Washington Post.*

"You're gonna do that *and* build a childcare center?"

He had to admit the childcare center was not going

to be easy.

"Maybe the childcare center was a bit much to ask for, just for an ass-fucking," she said, her brow furrowed.

He cradled the side of her head. "Hey, I'll make it happen. Your ass is well worth it."

"So am I going to owe you my ass a gazillion times now?"

"Only if you want to, love."

She smiled. "I do."

With a growl, he rolled her beneath him. Her noodles would have to wait.

Chapter Thirty Two

Music filled the Gordon Lee for Mayor campaign headquarters, and even though the results had not yet posted, the atmosphere on election night was generally festive.

"If Little Red and I hadn't gotten back together, I'd take a run at her," May said to Ben as they watched Kimani smiling and talking with Maybelle as she set up the refreshments.

May had flown out to support their uncle the last few days of the campaign.

"You better behave yourself," Ben warned.

"Don't you threaten me." May poked him in the chest. "I've got the goods on you, brother."

May didn't know half the things that went on during his run with a triad, but he wasn't about to bring it up.

He watched as May went over to talk to Kimani, pleased that his sister had taken an almost instant liking to Kimani. Overall, it had been a good week. The District Attorney had charged Jake Whitehurst and Vince Donato for aggravated kidnapping and aggravated assault. The District Attorney had also scheduled a grand jury proceeding to seek an indictment against the organizers of the Scarlet Auction. And Ben had a lead on a possible location for the childcare center he had promised Kimani.

His only disappointment was that Kimani was back to spending the nights at her own place because she didn't want to leave Marissa alone. He suspected a small part of her was still tentative about diving into a relationship with him with both feet.

"What do you mean we may not know who wins until days later?" May asked Uncle Gordon as they stood together shortly after the polls had closed.

"There are absentee and provisional ballots to be counted," Uncle Gordon explained. "With ranked choice voting, the process of crunching the numbers is a little more complicated."

"The Registrar is posting results," a campaign staffer announced.

They gathered around a computer. A loud cheer went up as the results were posted. Though Gordon did not receive a majority of the first place votes, he had a wide margin as the second choice candidate for most voters. Even with the number of outstanding ballots to be counted, the numbers looked to be in Gordon's favor.

Kimani turned to Ben. "So we did it?"

"The campaign consultant is crunching the numbers, but it seems so," Ben replied.

With a squeal, she threw her arms around him. He had never seen her in such a giddy state before. He liked it.

By ten o'clock that night all the candidates except the school boardmember, who had a remote chance of winning if 90% of the remaining ballots went her way, had conceded the race to Gordon. Gordon gave a brief speech thanking his family and supporters. A number of people wanted to stick around to watch the election results for other races and continue partying.

But Ben had plans to spend the rest of the night at The Lair.

"What's this?" Kimani asked as Bataar drove them into the city. She unwrapped the box in her lap.

"Something to replace the wristbands," he answered.

She lifted the lid to find a leather choker studded with small diamonds. The collar also had a metal circle for a leash attachment. Because of the gemstones, it was not the sort of gift Kimani liked to accept from him.

Knowing there was a high chance she would reject it, Ben felt strangely nervous.

"Will you wear it for me?" he asked.

She stared at it. "It's beautiful, but..."

Shit. He shouldn't have opted for the diamonds.

She turned her stare from the collar to him. "I'd love to."

His chest swelled, and he was able to breathe again.

He knew he had to give her space, especially given all that she had been through and all that was yet to come. But soon, she would be all his.

Not just for a week. But for the rest of time.

EXCERPT:
MASTERING THE MARCHIONESS

BESTSELLING AUTHOR
EM BROWN

MASTERING
THE
MARCHIONESS
CAVERN OF PLEASURES
Book One

Chapter One

HANGING FROM A HOOK, her toes barely touched the floor. Instead of the mask worn by many of the other guests at Madame Botreaux's Cavern of Pleasures, the young woman wore only a silk red blindfold. The rest of her was laid bare for all to see.

Vale Montressor Aubrey, the third Marquess of Dunnesford, circled around her like a predator examining its prey, occasionally running the tip of a riding crop languidly over her nipples. Once or twice he pulled the riding crop back and flicked it against a breast. She gasped, then groaned.

"Please...please, Master..." she pleaded.

Peering at her thighs through his black and silver mask, Vale saw the telltale glisten of moisture at her mons. This one never took long.

"Your punishment has hardly begun, m'dear," Vale told her.

"Please...forgive me...I was weak."

Suppressing a sigh, Vale pulled back the crop and lashed it at her buttocks. It was unfortunate. Her body was beautiful—with full ripe breasts that quivered when punished—but she had indeed proven weak.

"I leave you to contemplate how you can do better," Vale said with another swat of the crop.

As he headed toward the stairs, past a number of men and women engaged in various forms of coupling, a masked woman threw herself at his feet.

"Take me—I would be a far better submissive than she," the woman declared.

Vale looked down at her. His half-mask did not cover his frown or the hard set of his jaw, and she crept away in shame.

"Pray tell that is not boredom writ on your face?" asked Lance Duport when Vale joined his friend and Madame Botreaux in the balcony from where they could view the activity below, much like patrons in an opera box.

It was the favorite spot of Penelope Botreaux. She rarely ventured onto the floor of the *Cavern of Pleasures*—so-called because the large assembly area existed practically in the basement of her residence. Unfinished walls left the ground rock exposed. As there were no windows, only the dim glow of a few strategically placed candelabras penetrated the darkness.

"I let you have the beauty when I could have made her mine," Penelope declared from the settee upon which she lounged like a Grecian goddess, wearing a thin transparent gown over a body that time and a few too many glasses of ratafia had made plump in various places.

"I regret your generosity is wasted on me," Vale replied, removing his mask and looking over the balcony to where he had left the young woman.

"Perhaps I am too old for her."

Penelope snorted. "I am over forty and hardly consider myself old. You are barely five and thirty."

"And you could best any of the younger men here," added Lance as he raked an appreciative gaze over Vale's body.

An active life of riding, hunting, fencing, and an occasional bout in the ring kept Vale's physique in admirable shape. His stockings encased calves that were the envy of his peers. His simple linen shirt opened to reveal a broad, strong chest. His tight breeches covered muscular thighs and left little to the imagination.

Lance turned to Penelope. "You know half the women here—and men—would give their right buttock to be partnered with Vale. He needs more than a neophyte."

"Would *you* give your right buttock?" Penelope returned.

Lance curled his thin lips into a salacious grin. "I would give *both* my buttocks. Do you remember Demarco?"

"Ah, yes, how can I not? He was a beautiful brute. A Samson with that lush head of hair."

"And cocky as hell, but Vale had him writhing in submission within the hour. After such a conquest, I wonder that Vale should wish to trifle with the weaker sex."

Vale smiled. "Despite all appearances, women are not the weaker sex."

"Well, what the devil are you looking for?" Penelope prodded. "Apparently not men, nor women of unsurpassed beauty. You have spurned *both* novice and skilled submissives. Only Lovell Elroy has had more partners than you."

Vale pressed his lips into a grim line as he looked over the balcony at a man wearing a red mask flogging a woman. "Lovell is malicious. He cares nothing for the women he is with. I wish you would throw him out, Penelope."

"But the women flock to him—especially those whose hearts you have broken."

"Lovell breaks more than hearts, Penelope."

"Ah well, like you, he is a beautiful specimen to behold, and I do enjoy beauty." Penelope held up her quizzing glass and blatantly directed her gaze at Vale's crotch.

"Egad, Vale," Lance interjected. "Nearly forgot: felicitations to you on your recent nuptials."

Vale started. He had nearly forgotten that he was now married.

"Indeed," Penelope said. "Where are you hiding this wife of yours?"

"We arrived in town but yesterday," Vale answered. "She is with my cousin Charlotte at the moment."

He was not particularly interested in pursuing the subject. Though he was sure that Charlotte would prove better company for Harrietta than he, he nonetheless felt a stab of guilt for pawning his wife off on a relative for the evening.

"And will you be introducing us to her?"

"Good God, no," Vale shot back. "She is a simple girl from the country."

"Hardly sounds like the sort of woman you would choose to marry after all these years," Lance commented.

Vale shrugged. "Dunnesford needs an heir. Does it really matter whom I marry?"

"Yes, but of all the beautiful and wealthy women setting their caps at you, why a chit for whom you seem to have ambivalent feelings?"

"Her brother and I were the best of friends before he died at Yorktown in the service of His Majesty. We served in the same regiment for some time together, and I owe my life to him. At the age of ten, I would have drowned in the lake at Dunnesford but for his efforts." Vale put back his mask. "I should return to the beauty. Her arms must be sore."

"Even if her constitution is weak," Penelope attempted, "her arse must be a delight. I almost wish I were a man that I might experience the feeling of being inside her."

Her arse should have been delightful, Vale thought as he recalled how easily his cock had slid into the woman due to the immense amount of wetness that had dripped from her cunnie into her sphincter earlier. But there had been something missing with this one—as there had been with all the others. The women were more and more beautiful, yet his drive, his passion, continued to diminish. Perhaps it was only natural once one had experienced all there was to experience, tasted all that a feast could offer.

"Ah, we have some newcomers," Lance noted of a few people who had just walked onto the assembly floor. "Damn me, that brunette looks like Charlotte, but who is the one next to her with the lackluster brown hair and emerald necklace?"

Vale narrowed his eyes at the three emeralds separated by two small diamonds and laced together with silver. At first, he paled. Then his jaw hardened as he answered, "My wife."

Chapter Two

FOR HARRIETTA DELANEY, now Marchioness of Dunnesford, the eye holes in her mask were not large enough to accommodate her wide-eyed stare as she followed Charlotte onto the floor of *Madame Botreaux's Cavern of Pleasures*. There were men and women about her in all states of undress, and yet she, clothed from head to toe in a modest evening dress, felt like the naked one.

Not only were these men and women openly naked *in public* but they were engaged in all manner of...activity...*in public*. It hardly seemed real. Only in her fantasies—deep, dark fantasies that she had never shared with anyone—had she envisioned such possibilities. Only in London could such a place exist. Certainly not in the small town where she had lived for all four and twenty years of her life. The prospect of living in the City had been the one bright part of marrying the Marquess of Dunnesford. It was a marriage that made her among the luckiest women in England. And the biggest fool.

"He has wealth and breeding and a title *and* is pleasing to the eye," Bethany, Harrietta's junior by four years, had cooed after the Marquess had finally accepted one of their mother's numerous invitations.

"*Exceedingly* handsome," Marianne, who had yet

to have her come-out, had sighed.

Even Jacqueline, the youngest Delaney daughter at twelve, had agreed. "He looks like a *prince.*"

Harrietta had to admit that King George himself was unlikely to have produced as grand an entry as the Marquess, arriving in his gilded carriage pulled by a team of four with gleaming white coats and footmen who appeared to possess more expensive garments than the wealthiest of the bourgeoisie. The Marquess was also perfection, from the finely powdered hair to the elaborate cravat tied at his throat, the rich velvet coat that flared from the hips, his delicately embroidered waistcoat, and down to the jeweled high-heeled shoes. He was elegant yet commanding. Powerful but refined. Regal and sensuous.

Nine long years had passed since she had last seen Vale, and she no longer recognized him. She had dreamt of him, still flushed when she remembered their last encounter, and had heard much about him—especially about the many mistresses he had kept in those years. At the time of her marriage to him, he had been most recently rumored to be with an Italian countess. A family friend who traveled in the same social circles as the Marquess had described him as an aloof and arrogant rake—not the sort of man Harrietta had ever envisioned herself marrying.

The Marquess was a stranger to her. He was not the Vale who once preferred the company of the Delaney family to his own, who had been Harold's best friend, and who had been like a second brother to her.

She resented this magnificent Marquess for failing to be the man she had fallen in love with as a girl. But Mr. Delaney had three daughters with no dowries. That a man of Lord Dunnesford's stature would offer for Harrietta—poor and plain—was, according to Bethany, nothing short of the most miraculous gift Fate could bestow.

Dear God, Harrietta thought to herself as she glimpsed a woman whose breasts were being serviced by the mouths of two different men, *surely I belong in Bedlam for wanting to see this place?*

What she saw next answered her question affirmatively. A naked young woman was hanging from a hook like a slab of meat in a butcher's shop while a man wearing a silver and black mask was circling around her—and striking her with his riding crop. Harrietta had never seen such tight breeches as those worn by the masked man. She flushed on his behalf. Her gaze traveled from his loins to his finely sculpted chest. The sinews of his strong arms revealed themselves as he pulled the crop back and lashed it against the woman's backside. Harrietta eyed the planes of his pectoral muscles, the ridges that filled his torso, and the rugged hardness of his belly. She had not thought the naked body of a man could be so...captivating. The man would have made an exceptional model for Michelangelo.

"Masterful, is he not?" Charlotte whispered.

"What is he doing to that poor woman?" Harrietta asked, appalled yet intrigued.

"Punishing her. She has displeased him in some way."

The young woman groaned...in pleasure. Harrietta felt warmth spreading through her body. Her own carnal experiences had been limited to a few encounters with the footman and the squire's son. There had been groping—a few playful swats on the butt that she had surprisingly enjoyed—but nothing on the order of what she now witnessed. But she had imagined a world of greater possibilities ever since she had found a copy of *Fanny Hill* that Harold had hidden beneath his bed.

"He is the most desired master," Charlotte explained. "Only the most beautiful and practiced are selected to be his submissive."

"Have you ever been with him?" inquired Harrietta as she followed the hard set of his jaw. "I should think it rather terrifying."

Charlotte closed her eyes and a small smile played upon her lips. "I would be unworthy."

Harrietta studied her companion, who seemed to be reveling in a daydream. She liked Charlotte—and not because the woman was her only friend in London at the moment. Widowed two years ago, before she had turned thirty, Charlotte Kensington possessed a worldliness and self-assurance that Harrietta appreciated. It therefore surprised her that Charlotte would want to submit to a man like the one in the silver and black mask.

When she saw the man leave the assembly floor,

Harrietta felt relieved, though she was also curious to see what he might do next with the woman he had left hanging.

"If you wish to leave, you have only to speak it," Charlotte said.

Harrietta contemplated the suggestion. She had seen more tonight than she had ever thought possible. Her mind whirled and she needed time alone to digest all that she saw. And yet, she felt a part of her awakening, a part of her that desired to see more, a part of her that was not merely curious.

"Does everyone wear a mask?" Harrietta asked, stalling.

"Mostly," Charlotte replied.

"Do you know anyone here?"

"No, and that is part of the fun."

They walked past a row of semi-private alcoves occupied alternately by two women licking each other, a group orgy, and a ménage-a-trois.

"Are there no private chambers?"

"Where is the thrill in a private chamber? Ah, it is the time for presenting," Charlotte observed of a number of men and women who had begun forming a line in the middle of the assembly. "Did you wish to present tonight?"

"Present?" Harrietta echoed. Her pulse began to quicken.

"Those new to Madame Botreaux's must first present themselves. Those of a certain seniority here are allowed to choose among the new ones."

"What happens if you do not like the person you are with?"

"If you find you do not enjoy your initial encounter, you may request to present again upon your return."

Harrietta's heart was pounding in her head. For a brief moment she wondered what her new husband would say or do if he ever found out what she had done. He had made it quite clear before they married that he would not interfere in the life she wished to lead if she would afford him the same consideration. The coolness of his tone as he spoke had surprised her. In truth, she had felt a little stung by it. She knew full well she was not the sort of woman to merit the attentions of a man of his wealth and stature. That he had offered for her hand had mystified her. She could only guess that he had felt some obligation to her brother to care for his family.

He was certainly not interested in *her*. That much had become clear as crystal to her when he had chosen not to consummate their marriage on their wedding night. Instead, he had adopted a fatherly tone, assuring her that he would not press his privileges upon her but would wait until she was ready. What the bloody hell could he have met by that? The only answer that came to her was that he had no desire to bed her. Her lack of beauty had never bothered her before—Harold had often told her how he would sooner be in her company than all the Helens of Troy in the world—but on her wedding night, she had felt the pain of her plainness.

It was possible that despite the understanding that she and the Marquess had not to interfere in each other's lives, this would be too much for him to accept. *But why should he have all the fun?* Harrietta found herself reasoning as she thought of the Marquess with his mistress. Moreover, her identity was protected by her mask, and she trusted Charlotte not to divulge their illicit tryst. He would never know.

The man in the silver and black mask had returned and released the young woman from her bonds and her blindfold. He said something to her that made her cry. At first Harrietta thought he was telling the woman how much more she would be punished, but then he gently wiped away the tears from her face, and his lips formed what seemed to be the word *adieu*. The woman departed with obvious reluctance, casting one last look of longing at him before she left.

What would it feel like to want to be with someone that much? Harrietta wondered.

"If you worry that Vale—" Charlotte began.

Harrietta was quick to dismiss the suggestion. "Not at all. One of the maidservants mentioned that he is likely to be at the home of his mistress, the Countess D'Alessio. I suspect he will not return for some time."

"Does that mean you wish to present?"

For some reason, the thought of her husband with his mistress spurred her courage. "Yes—for tonight."

"Very well. I will wait for you when you are

done."

I have lost my mind, Harrietta said to herself as she stepped into the line formed by four other women and three men. She could not deny that her body felt warm from seeing all the bodies of men and women writhing in pleasure, but she had not expected that she might be one of them tonight. From the corners of her eyes, she saw the man in the silver and black mask, his arms crossed over his chest as he looked over the line of men and women presenting. She wanted to flee.

But then she saw him move. He was coming toward her.

Chapter Three

VALE SAW LOVELL ELROY, a man equal to him in physique and dominance, saunter toward the line of newcomers. It was unlikely that Lovell would select Harrietta—if the man selected anyone at all. Not all newcomers merited a partner. And Harrietta, with her square shoulders, petite breasts, and common features, was not the type of woman who would catch Lovell's eye. But Vale couldn't take that chance.

Damn Charlotte, Vale thought, when I lay my hands upon her...

"You," he said to Harrietta in a hoarse whisper to disguise his voice. "Come with me."

Lovell looked over. The rivalry between him and Vale was understated but obvious. Vale knew that Lovell was wondering why he was bothering with someone like Harrietta.

Vale began walking away. The sooner he removed Harrietta the better. What the devil was Charlotte thinking bringing her here?

He realized he was not being followed and turned back. Harrietta had not moved. Instead, she simply stared at him dumbly.

"I will assume you did not hear me," Vale told her. Heads around them began to shake.

She glanced over to where Charlotte was standing. Charlotte nodded her head encouragingly.

"Come with me," Vale repeated and turned once more. This time Harrietta followed. He led her to the farthest and most private alcove. It was also one of the darkest, allowing him to reside in the shadows of the faint candlelight.

"Stand there," he directed her, pointing to the center of the room with his riding crop. He surveyed her evening dress. It was a simple gown of violet damask that was part of the new wardrobe he had purchased for her as part of her wedding gift. The corset had managed to push her petite breasts up to form faint contours above the décolletage. She wore her hair curled, but loose and pulled away from her face. The blue half-mask covered what he knew to be a pert little nose but not her full lips, which formed a slight frown in their state of rest. Vale shook his head. Why did she bother with a mask when her emerald necklace—a family heirloom he had presented to her on the day of their wedding—flashed around her neck like a beacon?

"That is a striking necklace, ma petite," he said as he ambled around her slowly.

She realized her error and stammered, "I—it belongs to a friend. She lent it to me for the evening."

An adequate lie, Vale thought to himself. He wanted to sigh and run his hand through his hair. But he continued to circle around her as she watched him cautiously. Why had she come? And what was he going to do with her now that she was here?

"You don't belong here," he pronounced.

She lifted her chin. "Indeed?"

"You had best return home with your friend."

"I will leave when I am ready."

Vale pressed his lips together in displeasure. He was well acquainted with her stubborn streak—one that she shared with Harold—and it seemed time had not diminished that quality. God, but she looked so much like her brother, Vale thought to himself as he studied her. The memory of his best friend tugged at his heart with fresh vigor in her presence. He could feel the guilt in every cell of his body. He should have tended to the Delaney family immediately upon learning of Harold's death. Or at least when he had assumed the title of Marquess and had come into his full inheritance. The Delaney family had provided him with the warmth and affection that he lacked from his own family. He owed them the courtesy of a visit and so much more. But each passing year only strengthened the inertia. The guilt grew until he could ignore it no longer, and he had thought to absolve himself by marrying Harrietta; a posthumous apology to Harold for not having taken better care of his best friend's family.

"This is no place for you," he told her.

"Who are you to judge?"

He stepped toward her. She jumped a little but remained where she was. He stood behind her and leaned in toward her ear.

"Did you think I could not smell your apprehension?"

"That is merely because I am unfamiliar here," she responded.

Vale raised his brows. "You have been to similar establishments before?"

A smile tugged at the corner of her lips. "You seem to know all. You tell me."

Vale stepped back to better observe her. Was she lying or possibly telling the truth? If the latter, he had greatly misjudged the country girl he had married. She was staring at him, and he stepped once more into the shadows.

"In the Cavern, you will always direct your gaze in front of you," he explained. "You are not to meet my gaze or look upon me unless I direct you to. You shall always address me as your 'lord' or 'master.' Failure to do so has consequences."

Why was he telling her this? Vale wondered to himself. Best to get her on her way. But her response stunned him: she laughed.

"And what have you done to merit such a title?" she asked.

Insolent chit. Vale could hardly believe he was having this conversation. "You...are clearly a novice or you would not have the audacity to question me. I have no patience for greenhorns."

"Then why did you choose me—my lord and master?"

He would have preferred she not have added

those last words, spoken with such mockery. Never had Vale encountered such impudence in the Cavern. He was almost tempted to punish her.

"Because others would not be so kind as to advise you of the prudent course, which is to return from whence you came."

"Kind?" Harrietta echoed. "And were you kind to that young woman you hung from the ceiling?"

A flush spread through Vale. So she had seen him with the beauty. How much had she seen? But it didn't matter. It wasn't as if she knew who he was. Not even Charlotte knew."She was being punished," Vale explained. "And perhaps you noticed that she was not exactly complaining."

Harrietta seemed to consider the matter, but returned with, "And who gave you the authority to punish her?"

"She did. The source of authority always comes from the submissive. All that I do is what she desires me to do."

"She desired for you to strike her with your riding crop?"

"Yes. With an experienced master, even acts that she fears, resents, and dislikes are ultimately ones she wants to happen."

"What was she being punished for?"

"Spending without permission."

At last he was able to silence her. Her brows were knit in thought.

"An experienced submissive would know to do

what she was told," Vale continued, "and would not forget to address her master as 'my lord,' as you have done—repeatedly."

Her voice wavered every slightly as she asked, "And what will you do with me—my lord?"

This time the words were spoken with more respect.

"Send you home," Vale answered.

She seemed disappointed.

"Madame Botreaux's is not a place for the faint of heart," Vale told her with the tenderness of a parent explaining what was best for a child. "It is understandable to be curious, but in here a person needs to be committed and possessed of a certain level of ... ability."

"What kind of ability?"

"That you need ask shows your lack of understanding. Return home, ma petite."

He began to walk away.

"Where can I obtain the requisite ability?" she asked.

Damn it, Vale swore. Would she not give up? He had no idea how to answer that question. Many years ago, he had taken the time to work with new submissives, but he no longer had any interest.

"Would you teach me, my lord?"

Vale whirled on his heels and strode over to her. She was more than a head shorter and had to lift her chin quite high to meet his gaze.

"You do not know what you ask, ma petite," he

warned.

"Stop speaking to me as if I were a child," she returned. "You know nothing of me, but have conceived some prejudice against me. Why?"

She was beginning to irritate him. If he lifted his mask to reveal his identity, perhaps he could scare her away.

"Because you are a child," Vale said. "Only a child would persist in asking foolish questions."

"And only an arrogant lout would persist in sending me away." She lowered her voice. "I could be better than any submissive you have had."

The quaintness of her delusion made him laugh, which made her cheeks redden in anger. "I do not mean to deride you, ma petite, but you have no notion of the challenges you face."

"Show me," she insisted.

"As I said, I've no patience for neophytes."

"Then tell me who has. Will the gentleman with the red mask—"

"No," Vale returned with such vehemence that she jumped back. "He has less patience than I."

"And perhaps less arrogance," she muttered.

Vale caught her jaw between his thumb and forefinger. "You tread in dangerous waters, ma petite. You have courage only because you are unaware of all that you do not know."

"I know more than you think."

"Do you? How many men have you lain with?"

"Is it breadth or depth that matters?" she

countered.

Vale would easily have wagered that she was still a virgin. "And how deep does your depth extend?"

"Deep enough."

"I will be the judge of that. Have you ever been fucked?"

Her eyes widened behind her mask, and her breath quickened. "Often."

Liar, he thought to himself, but decided to let it go for he had another question he could ask. He stepped away from her and pointed to a ring on her finger with his crop.

"You are married. Have you lain with your husband?"

"If I was interested in fucking my husband, would I be here?"

Vale nearly choked. The ungrateful little chit. He could have married any number of women—women of unsurpassed beauty or breeding or wealth. She could not have done better than a tradesman or perhaps a wealthy but aging merchant.

Containing his own feelings, he remarked, "You do not regard your husband highly."

She hesitated. "Once... now I find him indolent and useless."

"Is he old and homely?"

"I understand many find him attractive, but he is old."

Devil take it, Harrietta, thirty-four is hardly old. Vale collected himself and continued. "Do you think

305

him attractive?"

"His countenance is not displeasurable, but his beauty is marred by the lack of beauty in his soul."

Vale stared in disbelief. He had never heard himself spoken of so harshly—and certainly not to his face.

"As bad as that?" he asked.

She winced. "I did not mean to...well, he is not the man I would have freely chosen to marry."

For the first time, Vale wondered if he had done a disservice in offering for her hand. "Is there someone you would have preferred?"

"No."

Relief washed over him.

"We have a convenient arrangement in which neither is to intrude into the life of the other," she added. "We are civil to each other."

"Does he know you're here?"

"He would not care, I think."

Vale suppressed a snort.

"He has himself a mistress," she supplied.

His heart sank. Though her countenance remained stiff and she straightened her shoulders, something in her tone belied her stoicism. He felt an odd compulsion to assure her that all was not what it seemed.

"If you've no wish to instruct me, my lord," Harrietta continued, "it is of no consequence to me. I will find another who can."

Vale began to pace the room. He could not let

her go about her own devices and risk her landing in the hands of someone like Lovell.

He held out his riding crop and with its end, kissed a nipple through her gown. Pulling his wrist back, he made to strike her in that same spot. She gasped audibly, but to her credit, she did not shrink from him. The chit was determined.

"Very well," he relented. "I will give you one night and one night only, but I have three conditions. Failure to meet any of them will indicate that you are not suited to be my pupil. Indeed, you will not possess the mettle to be a member of Madame Botreaux's if you cannot perform these simple tasks. First, you will arrive alone. No friends, no chaperones, and certainly no husbands or lovers."

"Your second requisite, my lord?" Harrietta prompted.

"Your impatience displeases me. The second condition is that you will meet me no later than ten o'clock tomorrow night—"

"Not tomorrow night!"

"Interrupting one's master merits a sound punishment," he informed her. "I recommend against it in the future."

He smiled to himself, knowing full well that tomorrow night would prove difficult for her, for he had offered to take her to her very first opera, Le Nozze di Figaro by Mozart. Harrietta had been thrilled, for the Austrian composer was her favorite.

"I can do any night but tomorrow."

"The choice is not yours."

She bit her lower lip in thought. "Very well."

Taken aback, he stared at her. Surely she did not mean it? He continued, "You will come clothed in no other color but red."

"That were impossible."

"The punishment for failing to address me properly will be three lashes. I can assure you already that your first lesson will not be an easy one."

Her lips curled in a frown, and Vale felt satisfied. "Those are your conditions. Unless you are able to meet all of them, I suggest you think no more of this place. There are other diversions in London that will better suit you, ma petite."

He left her to her own thoughts, satisfied there was little chance that she could succeed. But his plan did little to address another concern of his: what had prompted her to come to Madame Botreaux's—and wish to stay? He thought about their wedding night and wondered if he had offended her somehow. He knew plenty of husbands who would rape their wives and consider it no offense. Surely she would consider him kind for not forcing his attentions upon her? He did not think he could even if he tried. For God's sake, she was Harold's little sister. Though she had grown much in the nine years since he had last seen her—no longer a girl but a woman now—he could not resist the urge to protect her.

They would have to mate as husband and wife at some point. Dunnesford needed an heir, and it was the passing of his father a year ago that had finally forced the matter of marriage upon Vale. He had lived most of his life with little to regard for his father and had joined the army to spite the domineering old man, but his father had surprised him.

"Forgive me for the poor father I have been," the former Marquess had said on his deathbed. "I would not reproach you for refusing to honor me with a grandson."

For a man who had developed a keen sense of the desires of women, Vale had neglected to consider that his wife had certain needs as well. Lustful needs. For a moment he considered all the young men he knew, but quickly dismissed each and every one of them as an unsuitable partner for Harrietta. He shook his head. What other husband would find himself seeking a paramour for his wife? But he had to find another means to satisfy her. One that did not entail Madame Botreaux's.

God, what a bloody mess.

For more, visit

www.erotichistoricals.com

OTHER WORKS BY EM BROWN

His For A Week Series
Bought
Ravaged
Tormented
Devastated

Erotic Contemporary Short Stories
Damien
And Damien Makes Four

Cavern of Pleasure Series
Mastering the Marchioness
Conquering the Countess
Binding the Baroness
Lord Barclay's Seduction

Red Chrysanthemum Stories
Master vs. Mistress
Master vs. Mistress: The Challenge Continues
Seducing the Master
Taking the Temptress
Master vs. Temptress: The Final Submission
A Wedding Night Submission
Punishing Miss Primrose, Parts I – XX
The Submission of Lady Pennington

Made in the USA
Las Vegas, NV
28 December 2021

39711205R00174